Brenda,
All the best

REX GOUDIE
IDOLIZED

REX GOUDIE
IDOLIZED

Kim Kielley
Foreword by Rex Goudie

CREATIVE PUBLISHERS

St. John's, Newfoundland and Labrador
2006

We gratefully acknowledge the financial support of The Canada Council for the Arts, the Government of Canada through the Book Publishing Industry Development Program (BPIDP), and the Government of Newfoundland and Labrador through the Department of Tourism, Culture and Recreation for our publishing program.

Cover Design: Todd Manning
Layout: Joanne Snook-Hann
Printed on acid-free paper

Published by
CREATIVE PUBLISHERS
an imprint of CREATIVE BOOK PUBLISHING
a division of Creative Printers and Publishers Limited
a Transcontinental associated company
P.O. Box 1815, Stn. C, St. John's, Newfoundland A1C 5P9

First Edition
Printed in Canada by:
TRANSCONTINENTAL PRINT

National Library of Canada Cataloguing in Publication

Kielley, Kim, 1963-
    Rex Goudie : Idolized / Kim Kielley.

ISBN 1-897174-13-6

    1. Goudie, Rex, 1985-. 2. Singers — Canada — Biography. I. Title.
ML420.G688K47 2006   782.42164'092   C2006-904162-8

TABLE OF CONTENTS

FOREWORD & DEDICATION
By Rex Goudie

When I first started this whole journey, there was no possible way I could have seen all of this happening.

A recording contract, a presumably platinum CD, (I still don't know for sure), a cross country and province tour. I still don't feel like it's real.

And now this book. I have to admit, I was a bit skeptical when I first heard the idea, didn't want to get all repetitive with what everybody had already heard.

Fearful, at the most, of over-exposure and of people getting sick of the same stories they've already heard, I met with Kim.

All fears were set aside. She told me that she felt I was "Idol'ed" out, so to speak. I was thinking, "Thank God." I knew from that point on that this could be a rewarding experience.

Kim met with my family, my teachers, a few fellers I worked with at Northco, and those who know me better than anyone, my true friends.

This is the story of my whole life, not just the last year. I'll admit, it's still a bit scary to have people know most of what I did in my life, but it's just as well. And some of the proceeds are going towards the SHARE Foundation. So it all helps.

I want to say 'Thank You' to Kim Kielley for making this experience a great one. Not only do I now have one more contact in St. John's, I have another friend.

Thanks for making this a good laugh — at times, a good cry — and an overwhelmingly good experience.

This is dedicated to those I've lost. Roy Goudie (Pop), Gwen Lane (Nan), Frank Lane (Pop), Rex Goudie (Uncle Rex), Bradley Shiner, Steve Knight and Maureen Dicks.

Rest in peace b'ys, break the trail for the rest of us.

… Rex

CHAPTER 1
THE OUTPORTS TOUR

And the crowd went *wild*.

The collective roar of thousands of fans filled Mile One Stadium in St. John's, Newfoundland, on June 23, 2006, when Rex Goudie stepped on the stage.

It was the first night of 'The Outports Tour' and Goudie was ready for the home-coming.

Wearing a green ball cap, two T-shirts, blue jeans, his signature wrist bands and a snappy looking watch, he casually moved forward with a glowing smile on his face.

Screaming fans applauded and hooted. Goudie was never their *Canadian Idol* runner up. To them, he was, and is, their icon.

His journey to this moment in time had taken just over three years and involved a lot of life experience.

When he was 16, he auditioned in St. John's for the 2003 TV reality show, *Pop Stars: The One*. It was his first such audition. Quiet and shyly peeking out from under long bangs, Goudie sang.

The judges were ruthless. When they were finished with the unassuming teen, Goudie quietly thanked them and left. His nervousness was apparently more powerful than his voice.

But now, standing on stage at Mile One Stadium and kicking off a tour of cities and towns across his home province, Goudie belted out tunes to an almost full house. It was his third time packing Mile One in less than a year.

The songs he sang were tunes on which he grew up. They were the cigarette smoke-tinged songs made famous by people like Tom Petty and Bruce Springsteen and groups such as Steppenwolf.

A year had passed since people first started hearing the name 'Rex Goudie.' He would come so close to winning *Canadian Idol*. An album was now out and he was starting his second tour. Life was sooo crazy. But this tour was Rex's way of giving back to the people who put him where he was today. "It's my fans' concert," he said the day before the show. "I needed to go to the people in the outports who couldn't get to the major centres in the province. That's why I'm doing what I'm doing. So they can get a chance to see me."

On this night, the fans' commitment to Goudie came in the form of bodies streaming into Mile One Stadium and insane screams. "We Love You Rex!" they bellowed from the stands.

Goudie sang for almost an hour-and-a-half. After the show seemed like it was over — even after the encore — it was just the singer and his guitar on stage, performing *Sam Hall*, a ballad he learned from the generations before him.

Practically every person in the audience sang along. From small children to senior citizens, people sang, swayed and smiled. Some even cried. Goudie was finally home. And he sang from his heart.

Why is the Boy from Burlington so tremendously popular? Why do little girls and big girls alike get giddy when he is around?

Maybe it's the way he tugged on his T-shirt in a charming, boyish way, smoothing imaginary creases while standing in front of thousands of people.

Perhaps it's the way he jumped off the stage and touched the outstretched fingertips of squealing fans or the way he stops everything to sign an autograph.

Or, possibly, it's because he's one of the good guys who's from 'home' and is doing well for himself.

Bags and bags of fan mail line Rex's closet. And that doesn't include the box his mother brought to him on a recent trip to Toronto.

During the first concert of the Outport tour, Goudie never sang out of tune or forgot the words to a song. He involved his audience. He gave them an encore. He did his absolute best.

The rest is history.

In less than a year, Rex Goudie went from 0 to 100, and erupted as a Canadian heart throb. But it's more than that.

Safely tucked away in the corner of his closet at his home in Burlington, Newfoundland, sit plastic bags stuffed to the brim with fan mail. The letters, cards, posters and photographs are from people across Canada.

One card, large in size, has neat, school girl-like writing inside. It's filled with warm wishes and greetings. All are expressions of support for him as he made his way through the *Canadian Idol* competition during the summer of 2005.

This card, however, is from a senior citizens home in Newfoundland. The school girl lettering likely belongs to a staff member writing on behalf of the residents.

It's a testament to the twenty-year-old's appeal. He is not the runner up of a national competition, whose future is unknown after his contract expires.

Rex Goudie is a Newfoundland icon. He is a true blue, honest to goodness, nice guy from an outport with a population of less than 400.

He is the boy next door. He comes from good people. He's the kid that mowed your lawn, walked your dog, or held open the door for you. He's the guy you'd want your sister or daughter to date.

He is Rex Goudie, singer, songwriter, mechanic, overall nice guy.

So whether it's standing on a stage in front of thousands of screaming fans or turning wrenches on his dad's dump trucks, Rex Goudie isn't going away any time soon.

Because nice guys do finish first.

And Goudie is one of them.

CHAPTER 2
'WE HAD A BABY. IT'S A BOY.'

Rex says this picture reminds him of a carburator. The air intake is at the top of his head and he's hooked up to all kinds of wires. Of course, that's not really the case. Rex was just hours old when this photo was taken. The little tyke almost didn't make it through the night. This is the only photo of Rex's days in an incubator.

After moving from Burlington to Tumbler Ridge, British Columbia, Tana and Dwight Goudie settled into the task of living and working in the small mining town in the '80s.

It was like a scene from the Wild Wild West. There were no houses or stores built. Tana and Dwight's house was the third basement poured in the community.

And they started their family.

Their first child, Ryan, weighed nine-and-a-half pounds when he entered the world at Dawson Creek, British Columbia. Tana resembled a weather balloon, Dwight recalls, remem

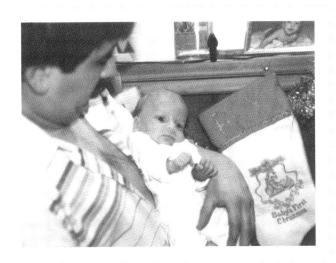

Rex's first Christmas.

bering how his tiny wife looked carrying their first child.

Ryan was a strapping youngster. Stocky and strong, he was the apple of his parents' eyes.

Then Tana and Dwight decided to have another child.

During the early months of that pregnancy, Tana had an emergency appendectomy. Doctors assured her all would be fine with her unborn child.

But as time went on, she noticed the baby did not move as much in the womb as Ryan did.

It worried her and Dwight.

And for good reason.

When Rex David Goudie entered the world on November 18, 1985, he weighed just over five pounds.

Dwight remembers just how tiny of an infant he was. "The nurse brought out the umbilical cord to me. And it was just a dead, white mass, except for one little thin red line about the size of a string."

Rex's skin was so thin, you could almost see through it, Dwight adds.

It did not look good for the baby. Dwight picked up the phone and called his mother, Lillian, back in Burlington. "Mom, we had another boy," he told her, his voice tired from the long night before. But he did not think his second child was going to make it through many more nights.

The doctors, however, could not believe baby Rex was doing so well.

"I left to go back to work," Dwight says. "Ryan was at home with his Aunt Trudy. When I got home, I had a phone call to come back."

Dwight raced back to the hospital in Dawson Creek. The doctors had

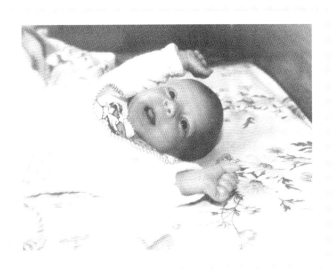

Rex was getting practice for his victory stance in this photo. He's likely used it a lot over the years, from his days playing hockey to his time on *Canadian Idol*.

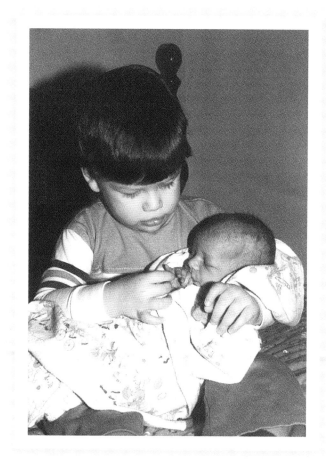

Rex can't be more than a few days old in this photo. Here, his big brother Ryan holds him after he came home from the hospital.

already prepared to fly Rex to a hospital in Vancouver. There were needles stuck in his head.

The sight startled Dwight. There were two doctors there waiting for the helicopter to arrive. Rex was only a few hours old.

Doctors told Tana and Dwight not to be surprised if their child had brain damage. He was not getting enough oxygen or sugar and his heart rate skyrocketed. "His levels went through the roof," Dwight says.

But the flight to Vancouver was too stressful on the little boy, so they landed in Prince George, a closer community, and waited it out.

Every day Rex gained an ounce, the Goudies would celebrate. When he lost weight, they were crestfallen.

All the while, they worried about Rex having brain damage.

For two weeks, Dwight and Tana were not sure if their second born was going to survive. And then, "he picked up, just like that. He came right around," Tana says. "There were no ill affects."

The doctors were amazed. They were baffled as to why Rex did not suffer brain damage. Maybe it was all the salt beef Newfoundlanders eat, they said. "And a mother's prayers," Dwight now says because Tana, to this day, hates salt beef.

For the next three years, the Goudies lived in Tumbler Ridge. After everything they had been through with Rex and having made the long trip back to Newfoundland every summer to spend their holidays, they felt it was time to return home and be closer to their family.

This is quite likely Rex's first ball cap. Though a far cry from the white one he wore during *Canadian Idol*, it's still a ball cap. His mom, Tana, smiles in the background.

Halloween at the Goudie household. Rex was still in diapers when this picture was taken.

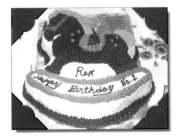

Rex's very first birthday cake, November 18, 1986. He was born November 18, 1985, in Dawson Creek, B.C.

The Goudies. Rex (on his mother's knee) is about six months old. Also pictured are Tana, Dwight and Ryan.

Rex (left) is about four in this picture. Ryan is about six.

Rex at roughly two years old. He still lived in Tumbler Ridge, British Columbia, when this photo was taken.

Hiya! Nothing worse than a karate choppin' baby. Rex, just barely walking, sports 'Kung Fu' baby jammies and does his best 'Flying Baby Dragon' stance.

CHAPTER 3
BACK TO BURLINGTON

Burlington, Newfoundland.

There's only one road that leads to Burlington and it's not paved.

Nestled at the end of Highway 413, just outside Baie Verte on the Baie Verte Peninsula, is Burlington, a place once called Northwest Arm.

In its day, Burlington was a lumber town.

Though isolated and at the very end of the line before land meets sea, the community lies on the north side of the mouth of Green Bay nestled in the folds of lush, green hills.

Frequent moose sightings at any time of year keep unfamiliar drivers to the town on their toes as they mosey down the road.

The view in the community is spectacular. Cool summer breezes blow lazily over ocean

This lighthouse was built by Alonso Saunders. It sits at the edge of the water as you enter Burlington.

Dwight Goudie (left) and Alonso Saunders stand in the 'Back in Time' museum in Burlington. Alonso's garage serves as the museum's home, the only collection of historical artifacts in Burlington.

water that sits in the harbour as the entrance to a town that unfolds like the beginning pages of a book.

Just at the mouth of the town, before you cross the bridge, is a lighthouse that jutts into the neck of the harbour like a beacon from days of old.

It belongs to a fisherman who almost lost his life on the water. Now he lives in a house where he converted his garage into the only museum in Burlington, the Back In Time Museum.

The lighthouse was built by Alonso Saunders, and it's inside his museum, a private collection, where the light for the lighthouse sits. It was given to Alonso by Rex's grandfather. There are other pieces from the Goudie family there amongst the artifacts of a town that once thrived. Alonso also purchased pieces from eBay and accepted donated items.

The door to the museum is always open. Just remember to sign his guest book. And don't forget to turn the lights off when you leave.

NAN AND POP LANE

After buying a piece of land in Burlington, Tana and Dwight started building a home. While they did, Tana's parents, Gwen and Frank Lane, looked after Ryan and Rex in Baie Verte.

It was the Lane's way of helping the young couple get started after spending so much time away.

A year went by. While Dwight and Tana were busy, Nan Lane, among other things, taught her grandsons to sing.

"Mom thought the world of Rex," Tana says. "She used to get him to sing to her." She always encouraged both grandkids to sing before they left.

"Sing Nan a song before you go," she'd say to Rex. And like the little bird he was, he'd dutifully chirp out a tune, enjoying the chance to sing for his doting grandmother.

When he was four, Rex found himself in front of a larger audience as he sang during Christmas concerts

Dinner at the Lanes. Rex and Ryan plant big, wet kisses on their Pop Lane's cheeks while their Nan Lane gets in on the act, too.

at the town hall in Burlington.

It was a family affair. The Goudie clan regularly organized the concerts to raise much-needed funds in the town.

The consensus with both the Goudies and the Lanes is that Nan Lane got Rex interested in music.

Gwen Lane played the pump organ. And she used to sing songs with the rest of the family gathered around her.

There was little surprise then when the first instrument Rex tried was the keyboard. Tana and Dwight put him in piano lessons, but the teacher told them shortly after to bring their child home. He couldn't teach Rex notes and scales. "(Rex) played by ear," Tana laughs.

There was no point to try and break that habit the teacher told her. Rex could play a song shortly after listening to it once or twice.

"He wanted to play guitar, but his fingers weren't big enough or strong enough just yet," says Tana.

As Rex got older, Gwen started suffering from Alzheimer's disease. It broke the hearts of family members to see their mother and grandmother, once vibrant and loving, fade into someone who didn't recognize them.

Rex and Ryan, always the dedicated grandchildren, visited their grandmother regularly with Tana. While hard on everyone, it was one of those things some families must go through.

Frank Lane was tireless in caring for his wife, even though she didn't recognize him.

While Frank was busy caring for Gwen, Rex and a friend would often go to Baie Verte during the summer and help with the chores.

One night while Dwight was away working in Labrador and Tana was at home with the boys, Frank suffered a fatal heart attack.

When the call came in the middle of the night, Tana piled Ryan and Rex in the car and headed down the Burlington highway towards Baie Verte hospital.

This is likely the first time Rex picked up a guitar. He's about three in this picture. Little did anyone know the instrument would become so important to him.

This is where Rex got his start, at the Goudie home in Burlington.

It was the middle of winter and they spun out twice, but nothing was going to stop them from getting to the hospital. Ambulance attendants were just bringing Frank into the hospital when Tana and the boys arrived.

The attending doctor approached Tana. He broke the news that her father had died. She let out a mournful wail. As she leaned over her father to say good-bye, she wrapped her arms around his big, burly chest. "He's still warm," she sniffed.

"Ryan couldn't take it anymore," Rex remembers. He hit the side of the rail that goes along the hallway in the hospital and broke it in half. "He doesn't know his own strength when he's mad," Rex says quietly.

Rex sang at his Pop Lane's funeral. Ryan played guitar with his back turned to the congregation because he's so shy.

Gwen eventually passed away too.

Rex sang at her funeral as well.

Before he started, he paid tribute to his grandmother. "When I was growing up, my grandmother used to say, 'Sing Nan a song before you go.' Before you go Nan, I'm going to sing you this song."

He sang *In the Garden*, her favorite hymn.

He didn't miss a beat. He kept his composure and sang it from beginning to end without wavering once.

Rex always seemed to have a musical instrument in his hands. Here he practises on his mother's keyboard.

There wasn't a dry eye in the church.

Rex did his best because, as he says, "If it's the last thing I'm ever going to do for this person, to show appreciation for everything they've done for me, I'll be darned if I'm going to mess it up."

CHAPTER 4
THE YOUNGER YEARS

It's bath time at the campground and a youthful Rex attempts to catch enough raindrops to fill the tub. Actually, Rex is just goofing around at a campsite with his parents in Newfoundland one summer.

You might think there wouldn't be anything to do in rural Newfoundland if all you knew was city life.

But not so.

There was always something on the go in Burlington. And it usually involved the outdoors. Summers were spent building forts, hiking, camping or shooting BB guns at targets.

Sometimes a BB would go astray and someone would get hit in the butt.

It stung, but not enough to stop the kids from going back the next day and doing it again. Sometimes they would play guns with out-stretched index fingers, yelling at the tops of their lungs, "Bang! Bang! Bang!" A big argument would erupt. "I shot ya!" "No, ya missed me!"

Who knew that one day Rex would make it to the 'Big League?' But instead of playing ball, he played a guitar.

There were a lot of good times, especially at a little cabin Rex and Ryan built behind their house. "We were painting it one day with rollers and spray cans," Rex recalls. "Just painting. I had a can of white spray paint and it wasn't working so Ryan took it.

"He flicked it and flicked it. But he couldn't get it to work. Finally, when it did work, it sprayed back in his face and he was covered in paint," Rex chuckles.

Parents in Burlington didn't worry about where their youngsters were. They knew if their kids were down the road playing ball hockey or baseball that someone was keeping a watchful eye on them. It was just something grown-ups did in the tight knit town.

Most of the kids Rex hung out with growing up did not have a lot of money. This was especially evident when they all gathered in the field behind Rex's place to play baseball.

When no one had a bat, someone took it in his head to carve a handle into a piece of two-by-four. It wasn't exactly a Louisville Slugger, but it did the job. The kids in the neighbourhood would then play a rowdy game of Wiffle ball rather than baseball.

The day Rex got a shiny red Cooper junior baseball bat was the day he was the most popular kid on the road.

He was so infatuated with baseball he even talked his mother into cashing in her Zellers points and buying him a full Toronto Blue Jays uniform.

He looked like any other kid at a baseball camp as he posed proudly for the camera. He loved that uniform.

Winters were spent trapping rabbits, snowmobiling or playing hockey on the outdoor rink just down the road. Winter, by far, was the most exciting time of year for Rex.

The day his parents gave him a 12 Elan snowmobile was the day Rex thought he'd died and gone to heaven. That little snow machine was the six-year-old's pride and joy. "I treasured that

This was Rex's first snowmobile, a 12 Horsepower Elan. Here he stands in the middle of a frozen pond in Burlington. He's about six in this photo.

thing more than anything," he says.

"Burlington was a great spot to grow up," Rex says. "There was so much freedom. Plus we had the protection of everybody knowing everybody. Nothing was ever gonna happen because everybody knew everyone."

The underlying current was always musical.

There was a time, when a five-year-old Rex spoke up at Sunday school. He told the children and his teacher they were singing off key. He then proceeded to sing for them in what he believed to be the correct key.

As a three or four-year-old, Rex would be outside making snow angels. Out of the blue, Dwight would hear music floating through the house. "What are you doing, Rex?" he'd called out. Rex would say he had a song in his head he just had to play.

Christmas concerts saw Rex singing with members of his family. Usually, there was some comic relief involved. More than once a Goudie male would dress up in something outrageously funny.

Dwight's brother, Rex, was notorious for getting dressed up and singing as a woman.

One year, no one had money for costumes. A lowly mop was butchered for a hairdo and Uncle Rex dressed like Rita MacNeil, lipstick and all, while other members of the Goudie clan dressed as the Men of the Deeps, the miners' choir.

While Uncle Rex sure made an ugly woman, the shows were always a hit in the small town. They always served the community well as a fund-raising event.

Rex snared his first rabbit when he was about seven years old.

RAW DOUGH AND 'QUIK'

Rex continued to sing for Nan Lane before he left her side, but it was his Nan Goudie (Lillian) who kept the house stocked with chocolate Quik and fresh bread. Occasionally, to this day, Rex still calls Nan Goudie when he's in town and asks if she has any homemade bread in the freezer. Sometimes she'll even put a little bread dough to one side because she knows 'Rexie' loves it.

Tana got to a point where she refused to buy Quik for Ryan and Rex. The milk the boys went through

Rex catches up on some reading before hitting the road in Burlington in search of 'The Great Pumpkin' and some treats on Halloween night.

Rex decided to get dressed up one day and convinced his mother to go for a walk. Rex asked his mother if people would wonder who he was. He got a great laugh out of it.

was phenomenal. They would drink three and four beer glasses of it a day. (And probably eat a huge bag of cookies to boot.) At one point, Dwight considered buying a dairy cow.

But Aunt Cindy bought Quik every time she went to St. John's and dropped it off at her mother's house for Rex and Ryan. Aunt Cindy always made a big deal over the boys.

Growing up in Burlington was magical and memorable. As Rex's song *One True Summer Night* says, "Hold onto this, you never know what you might miss…"

Long summers, hangin' with friends, trading dinkies with his buddy Corwin, chasing girls and wearing funny hats.

Life didn't get much better.

CHAPTER 5
WINTER WONDERLAND

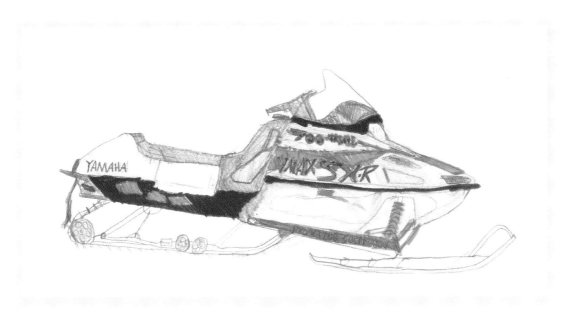

A snowmachine from Rex's personal sketch book.

It can take less than 24 hours to dump four feet of snow in Central Newfoundland.

Burlington is not too far from Corner Brook, which is a five-minute drive from some of the best skiing east of The Rockies (or so the ads say).

It's a snowmobiler's paradise in central Newfoundland. Groomed trails seem to go on forever.

In these parts, cabin owners don't board their little dwellings up for the season. They leave the doors unlocked and a stack of wood in the corner. Dishes and beds are at your fingertips. The only rule: if you use it, clean up after yourself and leave some wood indoors for the next crew.

It is an act of generosity, but also one of survival. Some folks maintain that snowmobiling in these parts is almost a religious experience, but when a freak snow storm whips up with no warning, being outdoors is not so enjoyable. It can be deadly. Shelter must be found immediately.

Knowing their cabin might mean the difference between life and death for some snowbound sole, many Newfoundlanders or Labradorians do not board their places up at the end of summer. They keep the doors open year round.

There are also shacks along the trail. These buildings do not have owners as such. They

Rex the artist drew some futuristic looking snowmobiles in his sketchbook during his childhood.

All geared up with someplace to go.

are just places to get out of the elements with a woodstove and some dry wood and kindling.

There is nothing like enjoying the snow and hospitality along the trails. Until you experience it, you will never come to realize why people in most of rural Newfoundland are almost fanatical about snowmobiling and their machines.

Rex is one of those fanatics. He loves snowmobiling. He was bitten by the bug early in life. Drawings of hybrid snow machines with flames shooting out the exhaust fill a sketchbook Rex doodled in as a kid.

And Ryan built his first snow machine at about twelve.

Out of frustration and the impending feeling his own machine was going to suffer a quick and painful death because the two boys were always on it, Dwight bought Ryan about four snowmobile skeletons. Some had good bodies. Some had good engine parts.

If you make it, they will come. Rex sits on a snowmobile at his parent's cabin covered in bread. As he sat perfectly still, birds landed on his arms and head to eat the bread he put out for them.

Dwight told Ryan that if he wanted his own snowmobile, he would have to make one out of the parts. And the eldest Goudie boy did it. "That taught him an awful lot, I think," Dwight says.

It was not until Rex was heading to Spain during the fall of 2001 that he got his first new snowmobile.

Tana calls it his "bribery" machine.

As the story goes, Rex had raised a fair chunk of money to go on a school field trip to Spain. He was excited to go.

But then the September 11 terrorist bombings happened in the United States and changed a lot of things, including Rex's school trip. Tana didn't want him to go to Europe. Rex was devastated. He had raised so much money for his first European adventure.

They agreed they would take the money from the cancelled trip, place it on the snowmobile of Rex's choice and pay the difference.

Tana and Dwight explained to Rex that once the decision was made, there was no turning back or regretting the decision.

Rex jumped at it. "Can I pick it out?" he asked his mother, expecting her to say no. But she did not and Rex chose a black and yellow Bombardier MXZ 550.

Rex always adored Bombardier products. So much so that his dream, once he got out of school, was to work for the Quebec-based firm.

But when Quebec was considering separation from Canada, Rex said, "Dad, that means if Quebec separates, I'm going to have to move to another country to do what I want to do."

Winter time saw Rex and his snow machine go everywhere. He and his very best friend, Ceilia Noble, spent hours snowmobiling in the countryside. When the friends got together, they would go for a trail ride over to the Goudie cabin, have a 'boil-up,'(a cup of tea boiled over an open fire) get warm and head back home.

 Just good old-fashioned fun.

During his last year of high school in nearby Middle Arm, Rex used his machine when the buses were not running due to bad weather.

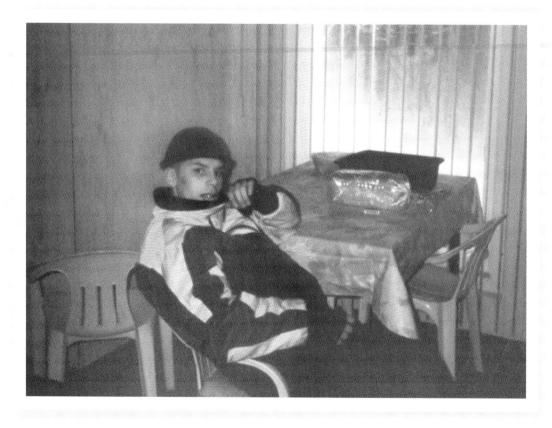

Rex relaxes at his parent's cabin before hitting the trails.

This is Rex's 'baby.' 'She' sits in his parents' garage in Burlington.

He was taking an advanced math course on-line with another person. If he missed just one day, it hurt his mark.

On those cold, blustery snow days, when the weather was too bad for the buses, Rex fired up his baby and made the trek to the school to do his math course.

To this day, the 550 Bombardier sits in Rex's parents' shed, shined and polished, waiting for winter to arrive and for Rex to come home and drive it like it was meant to be driven.

CHAPTER 6
HE SHOOTS ... HE SCORES!

Rex's love of sports carried itself over into his sketchbook.

Winters in Burlington did not only involve tracks, skis and snow for Rex.

It included watching a gazillion Toronto Maple Leaf hockey games.

Rex was interested in hockey from the day he could talk.

That likely stems from the Goudies and the Lanes, suggests Dwight. He played hockey. His brothers Mark and Rex did too, as did Tana's brother Terry. Then there were all the other sports Rex loved to play. Basketball, track and field... anything sports related, Rex was involved in it.

Felix Potvin, the Leafs goalie in 1992, was Rex's idol. Many hours were wiled away, hanging on the edge of his seat, watching Potvin's every move.

His Uncle Mark was a willing player. On the deck or out in the yard, he was always ready to take shots at Rex's net. Mark recalls firing a shot one time when little Rex was playing between the pipes like his idol Potvin.

"He wasn't wearing a jock that day," says Mark, and the puck hit Rex in the 'soft spot.' "Rex came after me, kicking and hitting. He was major peeved off. The tears were just streaming down his face."

Rex proudly displays his very first Toronto Maple Leafs jersey.

It just doesn't get much better than this. Rex got his Toronto Maple Leafs goalie mask for Christmas when he was about eight or nine years old.

Rex is right where he wants to be: in goal, wearing his Toronto Maple Leafs paraphernalia. Little did he know he'd be going to Toronto eventually, but not with the Leafs.

However, Mark, who spent a lot of time with Rex and Ryan while Dwight was away at work during the week, told Rex goal was the spot for him.

When Rex was around fourteen or fifteen, he traveled to Deer Lake for hockey school. He loved it and has the certificates and awards to prove it.

As geeky as his braces made him feel, if it wasn't for the face full of metal, Rex's brilliant straight smile might actually have been crooked and broken.

Once he got a hockey stick in the mouth and the force behind it actually moved his teeth back about a quarter of an inch.

"And then, after about a week, they just moved back in," Tana marvels. "I didn't know what to do. The dentist said they'll probably move back."

Rex still has his childhood goalie mask. Blue and

white, bent and dented in a few places, he will never get rid of the cherished treasure.

And hockey is a sport that will never leave Rex. Everywhere he goes, he drags his hockey bag with him, just itching for a chance to play with whoever wants to slap a puck around.

After *Canadian Idol,* one of the first things Rex bought with some of his 'new' money was goalie equipment.

However, it wasn't brand new. He bought it at a second hand store.

Since moving to Toronto after *Canadian Idol,* Rex has started chasing pucks with some good ole Canadian boys. Ironically, they're all associated with the entertainment industry, but they all play like the kids they once were except for now, they can afford new equipment.

There is a flood of childhood memories every time Rex laces up a pair of skates.

It reminds him of home.

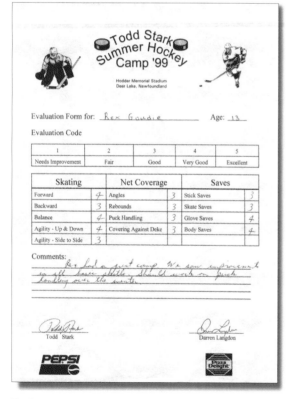

Evaluation report for Rex – 1999 (13 years old).

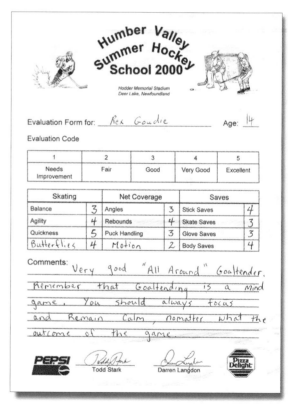

Evaluation report for Rex – 2000 (14 years old).

Rex at hockey school in Deer Lake with NHLer Darren Langdon.

Town of Baie Verte

Tel: 709-532-8222   Fax: 709-532-4134

P.O. BOX 218, BAIE VERTE, NEWFOUNDLAND
A0K 1B0

April 16, 2002

Rex Goudie
c/o Dwight Goudie
Burlington, NF
A0K 1S0

Dear Rex:

On behalf of council & the citizens of the Town of Baie Verte, I congratulate you & your team on having won the Bronze medal.

This achievement has no doubt been the result of hard work & dedication   As a town, we are very proud of the achievements of our athletes & feel honoured that you have won.

Yours sincerely,

Gus Roberts
Mayor

Rex was a participant in summer hockey camps growing up. He loved goaltending more than anything. Felix Potvin of the Toronto Maple Leafs was/is his idol.

Rex in the Hockey Hall of Fame beside the Stanley Cup. This is heaven for Rex.

CHAPTER 7
SCHOOL DAZE

Rex was on his way to Kindergarten and Ryan off to Grade Two when this photo was taken.

Rex was just a little fella in school.

And that made it tough for him.

His schooling started at Greenwood Elementary in Burlington. He went from Kindergarten to Grade Three there. It was then onto MW Jeans Academy for Grades Four to Six and MSB Regional Academy in Middle Arm for Grades Seven to Twelve.

Rex's brother Ryan went to the same schools. He was so much bigger than his little brother was and, generally, no one picked on Rex. They feared the wrath of Ryan. Still, Ryan did his best to let his little brother fight his own battles.

Garland Morris, Rex's Grade Five and Six teacher, lived a couple of doors down from the Goudies. Once Rex ended up in his class, it didn't take long for the teacher to realize the youngster was intelligent.

"Things came easy to him. He was a superb reader and writer," Garland recalls.

Throughout primary and elementary school, Rex was going to be a hockey player.

"Goalie was his thing," Garland says. "(Felix) Potvin was his number one idol."

And, of course, he remembers Rex always in net, just like Potvin. Sometimes Rex took things too seriously. At times playing hockey for fun just wasn't going to happen. Rex played for keeps. He played like the big boys.

But, like Garland says, hockey was going to be Rex's life. "That's what he wanted to play."

Even though he was a bright kid, it was not always easy to get Rex interested in school. He was a bit of a slacker who pulled off high marks with little effort.

And he was a little bit of a scrapper, too, Garland says. From Kindergarten to around Grade Four, Rex and another guy in his class fought regularly. Actually he drove Rex bananas, says Garland.

Dwight remembers one time in particular.

Rex went to school wearing a white Toronto Maple Leafs stocking cap he was quite proud of.

That afternoon, when he came home from school, the cap was white no more. And covered in mud, the cap was no longer a source of pride for Rex. His face was scratched as well, from a fight on the bus ride home.

Rex explained to Dwight that a fella in school had taken his cap and thrown it in the mud. "Dad," he said, "that kind of stuff really gets to me."

"So I told him, there's only one

Looking more like a university graduate, little Rex Goudie passed Kindergarten with flying colors.

way to fix this," Dwight recalls. "The next time that happens, you pop him right on the nose, right here."

With that, Dwight points to a spot on his nose.

"That'll fix that," Dwight told little Rex.

That afternoon, the school principal called. "Rex got off the bus and poked buddy right on top of the nose," said the exasperated principal. "I don't know what you're teaching your kids."

"I'm teaching him to stick up for himself. That's what I'm teaching him," Dwight told the principal.

"But you know, there were no problems after that," Dwight remembers. It was a tough lesson, but he thought Rex would be bullied forever if he did not learn to stick up for himself.

Then there was the time Rex broke a kid's nose at school.

"It was winter and we were flipping over the rail and into the snow," Rex recalls. "We thought it was good fun. So, this one day, the guy went to flip over and he got stuck. So I gave him a hand to help flip him over. He got mad at me for it and started kicking and hitting me. So I gave him one pop, right on top of the nose. I broke it and gave him a nosebleed. The teachers started freaking out at me. Everyone was saying I shouldn't have done it. But as soon as the teachers brought the kid in to get cleaned up, everyone turned around and slapped me on the back. 'Nice goin' Rex, b'y,' they all said."

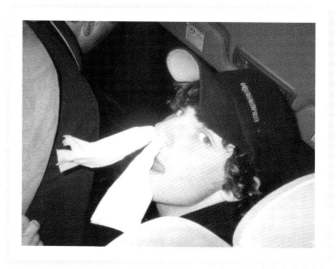

Warning: Don't try this at home. Oblivious to how this picture might impact his children many years later, Rex tries to clean his ears from the wrong end and winds up with wads of toilet paper stuck up his nose.

So frequent and expected were the fights that once they were over, Rex and the other fella would look at each other after a teacher broke them up and say, "Nice fight b'y, that was a good one.' " No hard feelings. That's just the way things were.

Garland Morris also remembers a spunky little kid who loved sports. "His heart and soul were 120 per cent into it."

When Rex showed up on *Canadian Idol,* Garland was surprised to see him, but certainly not surprised his former student tried out.

Garland remembered the little boy with a button accordion that sang and played for his Kindergarten and Grade One classes.

In 1995, Garland helped organize the big 'Come Home Year' celebration in Burlington.

Rex might have been nine or ten. He had decided he would sing for about 2,000 people. But he had about four or five pieces to sing at the concert.

One of the five songs was an old Newfoundland favorite, *The Loss of the Marion.* As Rex started, he confused the second chorus with the first and sang the wrong one. This was upsetting for little Rex.

As he started to cry, Dwight jumped on stage and whispered something in his ear, Garland remembers.

While Garland does not know what was said, Dwight does. "Rex," Dwight told him, "you don't have to do this if you don't want to. But if you really want to do this, just start over again and go. If you really want to, do it! If you don't, we'll go."

With that, Rex wiped his face, took a deep breath, and started from the beginning. Once he was done, the crowd enthusiastically applauded, showing their appreciation for a little boy's spunk.

Dwight and Tana have always tried to support their kids as much as possible, no matter what they were doing.

When Rex sang in front of 2,000 people that day, Dwight gave Rex a choice. He did the same thing during *Canadian Idol*.

"I said, 'The day you phone me and say you don't want to do this, I'll be right there to pick you up and get you the hell home out of it,' " Dwight recalls.

But Rex has never been a quitter, and was never one to accept defeat easily.

Despite this competitive nature, Garland Morris says Rex is the salt of the earth. He says Rex is concerned about people and wants to make a difference. While other kids were getting led astray, Garland says Rex was one kid who listened to his parents and took it to heart. "His family means everything to him," Garland says.

After retiring as a teacher, Garland moved from Burlington and settled just outside St. John's in Conception Bay South, the largest town in Newfoundland and Labrador.

Rex, dressed in his tuxedo for his Grade Twelve graduation at MSB Regional Academy High School in Baie Verte, Newfoundland.

To continue working, Garland started a company that provides security for various events throughout the St. John's region.

On the day Rex visited a St. John's Wal-Mart to sign autographs shortly after his album was released in the fall of 2005, Garland was there providing security for his former student.

They had come full circle.

Ironically, years before, as his teacher, Garland was there to help Rex further his education.

And now, as Rex sat in Wal-Mart signing autographs, Garland was there, once again looking out for his former student.

School Days

Rex, Grade One.

Rex and Ryan when Rex was in Grade
Two and Ryan was in Grade Four.

Rex, Grade Three.

Rex, Grade Four.

Rex, Grade Seven.

Rex, Grade Eight.

Rex, Grade Nine.

Rex, Grade Ten.

Rex, Grade Eleven.

Graduation

Rex graduates Grade Twelve.

Rex was a 'hat boy' long before Idol judge, Zack Werner stuck the name on him. Here Rex receives his Grade Twelve diploma.

Aunt Trudy loves Rex and Ryan like her own. Here, she planted a big red kiss on him before he left for his Grade Twelve graduation ceremony.

CHAPTER 8
FAMILY IS EVERYTHING

When Rex graduated from MSB Regional High School, his family gathered together to take this photo with him. From left to right, back row are: Dwight Goudie (Rex's dad), Tana Goudie, (Rex's mom), Trudy Sooley, (Rex's aunt), Rex, Issac Goudie (Rex's nephew) Ryan Goudie (Rex's brother) and Ruth Ann Goudie (Rex's sister in law). Front row: Roy Goudie (Rex's grandfather) and Lillian Goudie (Rex's grandmother).

If the Goudies are anything, they are close knit. When one of them is down or out, everyone drops what they're doing and comes running.

It's just that way.

So as Dwight worked on the road and Tana stayed home with Ryan and Rex, there were gaps that needed filling.

Usually it had to do with guy stuff. That is where Dwight's brothers, Mark and Peter, came in handy.

Dwight's brothers insured his boys were exposed to all sorts of sports in his absence.

There was never a shortage of Christmas presents at the Goudies.

The uncles and nephews were as close as any fathers and sons could be.

Uncle Mark is dry and witty. He is a straight shooter who doesn't mince words. He and Rex are on the phone constantly talking hockey.

Then there was Dwight's brother Rex. He was one of the funniest people you would ever want to meet, Mark says. "He'd torment you to death and always laugh at you."

Uncle Rex was a hulk of a man. With a bushy moustache, and a gentle face, he sang and joked at the Christmas concerts while members of the audience roared. A picture of one memorable event sits on the bookcase in Dwight and Tana's house.

Eventually, life on the road came to an end when Dwight decided he didn't want to be away from home anymore.

While Mark worked for the Department of Transportation as a snow plow operator, Rex, Dwight and Peter worked in the family trucking business and lumber mill.

It was as good as any relationship could be considering they were brothers working in a family business in an economically depressed area of Newfoundland and Labrador.

But they did their best and, for the most part, succeeded.

A low point came when Uncle Rex started experiencing headaches and went to Grand Falls-Windsor for a CAT (Computerized Axial Tomography) scan. The doctors discovered something blurry growing on his brain.

"They said he had a tumor growing on the stem of his brain," Dwight remembers.

Christmas in the Goudie household in Burlington. The big guy on his left is his brother Ryan.

It was more often than not that when Goudies gathered, people sang and played instruments. This time is no different. Here, Rex plays his button accordian while his Uncle Rex plays guitar.

Uncle Rex had an MRI (Magnetic Resonance Imaging) test at the Health Sciences Centre in St. John's.

"It didn't turn out to be that at all," Dwight remembers.

Apparently, his brother had a tumor on his pineal gland, which is deep in the centre of his brain.

When doctors in St. John's conducted a biopsy of the tumor, things went terribly wrong.

"Rex came out of surgery," Dwight says. "He was fine for a little while afterwards." Then the tumor on the pineal gland broke.

"Right next to that gland is the temperature zone for your body," Dwight remembers. "Rex's body temperature went to 45 degrees Celsius."

For the next four or five days, Dwight stayed by Rex's side. He tickled his feet and talked to him, but there was no response. Rex was in a coma.

Dwight and Gail, Rex's wife, did everything to get him to respond.

"They thought maybe he was brain dead," Dwight recalls. "His wife gave the go ahead to unhook him." Dwight swallows hard. He misses his brother Rex so much.

When Rex died, Dwight, Tana and Gail were by his side.

From the time Rex got sick, three months had gone by. It was 2004. He left behind his wife and two children, Lacey and Zack.

The Goudies were deeply affected by the loss. At his funeral, his namesake and nephew Rex sang *He Ain't Heavy, He's My Brother*.

Rex remembers an uncle who would cry when he sang the Harry Hibbs song, *Nobody's Child*, on the button accordion. It is such a sad, lonely song.

When Rex was in the Top 32 of the 2005 season of *Canadian Idol*, he decided to dedicate the song *After the Rain* to the memory of his uncle.

But he was not going to do it alone.

His plan was to pull a cheap lighter from his pocket, raise it over his head, and light it in memory of Uncle Rex.

He told the other Idol contestants of his plan and they agreed to go along with it, as long as he got them lighters.

Rex and the flameless lighter. He wasn't going to miss a chance to remember his 'Uncle Rex' on national T.V.

So, in true Goudie fashion — nothing was going to stop him once his mind was made up — Rex bounded across a busy Toronto street, over to the local hardware store, and bought a box of cheap lighters.

While some media said it was cheesy, Rex told his father it might be his only chance to be on national television and "I'm going to pay tribute to my Uncle Rex."

The morning of the show, Rex jumped out of bed and rifled through his belongings. Tana had flown in from Burlington and, when he saw her, he handed her something.

It was the name tag off the coveralls Uncle Rex wore when he drove the dump truck with Dwight.

Rex then handed Tana a work shirt and asked if she could sew Uncle Rex's name tag on it for the performance that night.

Everything was set. Uncle Rex's nametag was sewn on and ready. (Tana had a heck of a time finding a needle and thread in a hotel in downtown Toronto.)

The *Canadian Idol* kids had their lighters. Rex was ready to rock.

As the opening lines of *After the Rain* began, Rex reached in his pocket and fished out his lighter.

He raised his arm and, in typical cheap lighter fashion, it didn't work. But that did not stop Rex. He stood there, with his arm outstretched over his head holding the dead lighter like a torch. Only his family knew at the time why he did it on national television.

Behind him, the *Canadian Idol* contestants sat with one arm stretched over their heads, the flames of the cheap lighters flickering, for a man they never knew.

CHAPTER 9
WRENCHES AND SCHOOL

Rex always loved anything mechanical.

When he was little, he took one of Dwight's' books called *On Highway Trucks*, headed to the bathroom, and sat there for hours, figuring out gear ratios. Sometimes he even took the book to bed.

Then, he would take his sketch book and draw the gears.

His grandfather Lane owned a body shop in Baie Verte. Rex found an old car door lying around. For a laugh, he put on a little production for his parents that involved that door.

"He'd start, 'This is my car. This is how you roll down the window. This is my steering wheel.' He painted it, too," Tana laughs.

Pop Lane used to cut

This picture contains three of Rex's favorite things: a car, chocolate pudding and a view of the ocean.

snowmobile forms out of wood on his band saw for Rex. Then the boy would carve it.

Rex's sketchbook is chock full of drawings of hybrid snow machines and tractor trailers. And specs.

Rex brought home stacks of brochures from dealerships and read the specs of the different snow machines on the market. Ryan would look at a machine and size it up. But Rex knew the size of every carburator of every snow machine out there. "He knew everything about it," his dad says. "You'd be talking about machines and this little kid would pipe up and tell you everything."

When he got the chance to drive his father's '88 Ford L9000 tractor trailer in Grade 8, Rex was blown away.

Rex looks so happy. He's got a tractor trailer toy set and a model car to put together.

"I was watching Dad like a hawk. Everything he'd do," Rex says. "He let me take it out for a spin. That was fun. He trusted me."

At seventeen, he got his driver's license. "You're always trying to push the limits. Once, when I was coming around a turn and I caught some gravel with my tires, Dad got (phone) calls."

A '91 Camry with holes as big as his head was the car Rex found himself driving most. He constantly repaired it.

Deep down, Rex is a Ford and Bombardier man. It goes as far back as Dwight can remember. Even the fuzzy little caterpillars he let crawl up his arm were named Ford.

Erin Broderick, a good friend, deliberately wears her Polaris jacket to the Goudie household just to get a rise out of Rex.

It usually works and a good natured argument ensues.

There were two things Rex wanted to do. "I always wanted to do mechanic work or music. And at that time, I said, 'There's not much chance of the latter, but I could be pretty darn good at the former,'" he laughs.

Rex was off to college after graduating from high school.

"When (Dad) gave me the go ahead, I said, 'OK, I'll go to university and keep my standards up. I'll finish my courses and pass,' " Rex says.

And he tried. But chemistry was too tough for him. He was studying at Sir Wilfred Grenfell College in Corner Brook at the time.

He called his father and explained that school was not for him. He asked if he could work in the family business. Dwight agreed.

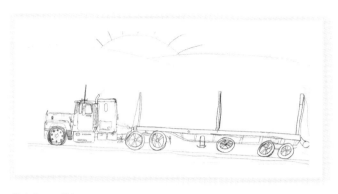

Driving off into the sunset with a tractor trailer of his own.

He worked Rex hard, never giving an inch, intent on teaching his youngest child that in the real world, it is all about hard work.

Ryan was working for the family business and going to school at the same time. With a baby on the way and no formal training, Ryan knew he had to get a good job to support his family.

Dwight continued working Rex hard until one day he announced he would like to return to school and study mechanical engineering.

It was the news for which Dwight and Tana were waiting. They knew their son would struggle if he did not have an education to fall back on.

He started at Memorial University in St. John's in January 2005. Tana's sister, Toby, ran a daycare from her home in Mount Pearl. She agreed to let her nephew stay at her house while he went to university.

Occasionally he stayed at his cousin Erin's house in St. John's to be closer to the university and 'The Breezeway.'

The Breezeway is Memorial University's famed bar. For the most part, it encourages 'Open Mic' entertainment. Rex jumped at the chance to perform in front of a crowd. With guitar in tow, Rex even worked his classes around the Open Mic schedule at The Breezeway.

"He used to ask for my approval when he stayed with me," says Toby. "I don't know why he asked because he was going to do what he wanted to anyway."

Once there was a huge snow storm. "Rex said, I think I'm gonna go down to the University tonight," Toby

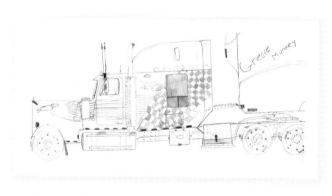

Another drawing from the sketchbook of Rex. This time it looks like his very own tractor trailer.

From dinkies to Mustangs. This is 'another Rex baby:' a black Mustang with red leather seats.

recounts. "And I said Rex, there's no way you're going out in that storm. The plows aren't even out." She finished the conversation with making him promise to call as soon as he got there.

Hours went by before Rex finally called. He apparently had waited a couple of hours in the storm for his taxi. Then, the taxi couldn't get through so he had to get out and push.

"And then we passed (the driver's) buddy and we had to help him out. So it

Not quite resembling his 2005 Mustang, this is a drawing of a futuristic car from Rex's sketch book.

took me a while to get there," Rex told his aunt. "But he never charged me."

Toby knows her nephew is willful.

"If he gets something in his head, there's no turning him," she adds.

CHAPTER 10
'BOXIE'

Rex playing guitar at age 3.

Some family members on the Lane side of the family still call Rex 'Box.'

He earned the handle at three or four when he could not pronounce 'Rex'.

"Me Box," was all he would say.

Erin Lane, Rex's first cousin, apparently chose the pseudonym and, to this day, at the Lane household in St. John's, Rex is stilled called 'Box' by his Aunt Von (Yvonne is her real name, but Rex couldn't pronounce that either), cousin Stacey and Erin.

It is a pet name more than anything.

Never without his guitar, Rex tagged along with Erin, who is three years older, whenever she went out with her friends who lived in Portugal Cove.

And when he did, her friends always wondered where Erin dragged Rex in from because he could play guitar and accordion and keep them entertained for hours.

Endless nights were spent sitting on beds and floors, gabbing away until the wee hours of the morning. Sometimes it drove Aunt Von a little crazy. She is an early riser. Rex is not.

Sometimes she would send Terry, her husband and Tana's brother, on her behalf, when Rex's guitar playing or gab sessions poked in past midnight.

Suffice to say Rex and Erin are tight. They are more than friends. They are blood. Erin says and does things to Rex that only someone related could get away with. And she knows exactly which buttons to push.

That's where Erin fits into Rex's life and Rex fits into Erin's.

It was April 2005.

Rex was staying at Erin's house while writing exams. It was just more convenient than staying with Aunt Toby in Mount Pearl.

Uncle Terry promised Tana that whenever possible, he'd keep a watchful eye on his nephew. So of course Rex could stay at their house during exams.

Erin had just come home and headed down the basement stairs to check on cousin Rex.

"Here he was with this book over his face, snoring!" Erin chuckles.

"What are you doing?" Erin demanded from Rex.

"I'm studying," came the sleepy reply.

"It looks like it," Erin said with a snuff.

She headed back upstairs to put on her pajamas. Heading downstairs once more, Erin discovered Rex fast asleep.

That's when she announced she had a 'surprise' for him.

She hauled a VHS tape off the shelf and popped it into the VCR. It was an old *Pop Stars: The One* tape.

"Oh Geez, turn that off," he blurted.

"And then he started getting mad," says Erin.

To coax him into watching the tape, Erin declared it would be good for a laugh.

On it, a sixteen-year-old Rex, stood in front of a panel of judges, including former *Much Music* VJ Erica Ehm. He sang and made it to the second round. But quiet and obviously terrified, Rex bombed.

"He was fuming," laughs Erin. "The judges said, 'You're sixteen. You're just here for the girls. You're not really into this.' He got sooo mad."

And then, Rex said the words Erin hoped to hear. "*Canadian Idol's* here. I got half a mind to go and try out for that."

Just a few musical instruments of Rex's. Check out his first guitar (centre), his button accordian and his mandolin.

It seems like Rex always had a guitar in his hands. Here he's playing electric guitar with an acoustic guitar on the bed behind him.

"I said, 'Go for it! Come on!' "

Egging Rex on, Erin kept pushing. "What's the worst that can happen to ya? They say no?" Rex was weakening. "I'll think about it."

He must have thought enough about it because the night before auditions, he stayed at Erin's house.

Wading through dozens of songs on the internet, he tried almost every one until his Uncle Terry hollered down the steps at him some time past midnight.

"Rex, b'y, I don't mean to put a damper on your enthusiasm, but you better put that away," he said. "You're gonna have everybody up in a minute."

Reluctantly, Rex packed up his guitar.

Toby remembers the list of questions he had to answer before going into the audition. "Rex thinks he's going to go all the way and he may not be able to make it for Ryan's wedding," she chuckled to husband Earle. "Rex, goin' all the way?"

07664

It's a number not many fans can forget as Rex kept his very first Idol number as a souvenir of the whole experience.

She did suggest, however, that Rex should go on George Street with a little band, but he told her he wasn't into that.

The next morning, at 7 a.m., Rex was in the *Canadian Idol* audition line up. While the people around him practised their songs, Rex studied for his exam in two days.

After making it through the first cut, he headed back to Erin's house. Another late night.

Bright and early the next day, Erin dropped Rex off at the second round of auditions. Wearing the same clothes as the day before because producers wanted it to look like auditions took place in one day, Rex stepped forward.

After singing Johnny Cash's *Folsom Prison Blues*, a song he sang dozens of times, Rex got what he was waiting for.

A gold ticket to Toronto.

With a beaming smile, Rex whirled around with the ticket in one hand. No one from his family was there to congratulate him.

But that was OK with Rex. He always had big dreams. And this time, he was one step closer to fulfilling them.

Walking back to Mount Pearl to his Aunt Toby's house — which, on a good day, would probably take eight hours — he connected with her on the side of the road. She was on her way to pick up the daycare kids.

He opened the van door and hauled something out of his knapsack. "Did you ever see a gold ticket before?" he asked his aunt.

And that was it. He was going to Toronto. Tana and Dwight didn't even know he was in the competition.

At first, Tana was upset. She thought Rex might be off on a wild goose chase. Then, the worry was how much it was going to cost them. She also thought about the education he was leaving behind.

But there was no changing Rex's mind.

Two of his best friends, Erin Broderick and Ceilia Noble, knew he was going to Toronto. He got on MSN to Erin and turned on his web cam. "Guess what!" he beamed at her. He didn't have to say a thing. He just held his gold ticket up. "I was so excited. I started to cry," Erin admits.

Erin and Ceilia told no one, not even their parents.

It was top secret.

CHAPTER 11
THERE ARE JUST SO MANY PAY PHONES IN NEWFOUNDLAND

A night at the mansion, Rex relaxes with his dad during the *Idol* competition.

What more can be said about Rex Goudie and the *Canadian Idol* experience?
You wonder if there is anything left that hasn't been reported or dissected to death.
Really, what more can anyone say?
In one word?
Lots.
And not from the competition stand point.
Rex, a small town Newfoundland boy with a charming smile that could melt any grandmother's heart, kept getting voted back on the popular reality show.
There were staggering ups and disheartening lows.

Through it all, Rex kept it together in a way that made his parents beam and an entire province proud.

Imagine how Newfoundlanders must have felt when one of their own stood on national television and wore the pink, white and green Republic of Newfoundland flag on his T-shirt for all of Canada to see.

It was a shout from the mountain top that said, 'Here I am. I'm a Newfoundlander and I'm darn proud of it,' despite Idol judge Zack Werner's unapologetic comment about requiring an interpreter to understand Rex.

The weeks in Toronto blended into each other.

Dwight and Tana vowed Rex would always have a familiar face in the crowd after the gold ticket incident. The troops circled the wagon. Friends who lived in southern Ontario made an effort to be at the show when Tana and Dwight could not. They also opened their homes and hearts to the Goudies. And family from Tumbler Ridge, B.C., made the trek to Toronto for the night of the grand finale.

This is where the *Canadian Idol* contestants hung out in the mansion during their off time during the competition.

Another hangout spot for the *Canadian Idol* contestants at the mansion.

But it all came with an expensive price tag.

As the numerous flights and hotel accommodations mounted, generous strangers handed over flights, hotel rooms and even meals for Tana and Dwight. There were so many acts of kindness that to this day the Goudies shake their heads and become almost speechless when they think about it.

Newfoundland followed 'their' boy from beginning to end, every Tuesday and Wednesday night.

As each week went by, Rex marveled at how his daily living allowance, outside of his clothing and food, kept increasing. At one point, he even tried to give the money back to the CTV person shelling out the cash to the contestants. He thought there had to be a mistake.

Rex had never seen that kind of money before. Then he made a little decision and, every week, he started squirreling away a few dollars to buy a left-handed guitar for big brother Ryan.

On the home front, while Rex sang his heart out in Toronto, family, friends and total strangers connected with one common goal: vote for Rex.

Everyone had their own techniques. Some were better at it than others.

Every Tuesday night, Erin Lane and her family in St. John's scattered as soon as Rex's performance on stage was over.

Due to the sheer volume of phone calls, home phone lines were unable to process the calls as quickly as pay phones. So Erin, Stacey, Yvonne and Terry went anywhere in St. John's where a pay phone was located.

In Mount Pearl, Toby and her family hopped into the van in search

This is the bed Rex slept in while he stayed at the mansion in Toronto.

of pay phones, sometimes before the end of *Canadian Idol*, setting the VCR to tape the show while they were out voting.

Rex's family members went all over the cities of St. John's and Mount Pearl to use the various pay phones. Some of their regular haunts were St. John's International Airport, The Holiday Inn, Memorial University, lobbies of local hospitals, and even RCMP Headquarters, where they sat for hours, pushing the same number repeatedly.

"We knew every pay phone in the city," Toby says.

At the airport, everyone knew there were eight pay phones. "So we took 'em all off the hooks and we'd start, 1-888-whatever. By the time we were finished the last one, the first one would be back up. And then we'd start again," says Erin.

Erin perfected the two-handed dial where she placed two receivers on her shoulders and dialed the number with both hands. Voting for Rex became at least a two-hour commitment.

Toby remembers a camping trip to Terra Nova National Park with her daughters and a family friend named Sandra.

They worked in shifts, dialing the number on the pay phone in the park. Mosquitoes chewed away at exposed flesh, but it did not matter as Toby and her gang voted for Rex.

Older people got caught up in the frenzy too. Sandra's mother would be in bed, the lights off, dialing in to vote on her cell phone. "Sandy's father caught her at it and said, 'For the love of God, would you give it up?' "Toby laughs.

Almost every pay phone in St. John's was busy with voters on Tuesday nights.

Family in Tumbler Ridge, British Columbia, and Fort McMurray, Alberta — where there are large concentrations of Newfoundlanders — supported Rex by posting signs around the two towns, encouraging residents to vote for Rex.

Voting for Rex on Tuesday nights became a coast-to-coast phenomenon.

Trudy Sooley, Tana's sister and another one of Rex's aunts, recruited friends and their business phones for voting.

Everyone, including Newfoundland and Labrador Premier Danny Williams, was rooting for Rex. He was in the audience during the grand finale.

In Burlington, it was a guarantee that every Goudie household in the community brimmed with friends and family supporting Rex.

POP GOUDIE AND STEVIE WONDER

Roy Goudie, Rex's grandfather, always made a point of either watching the show at Dwight's house or getting the scoop on Rex's performance Wednesday mornings.

On Monday mornings, Dwight was usually working in his garage on a truck. "Dad would come out and ask, 'What's he singin' this week?' or 'What's goin' on this week?' " he says.

"I told Dad I didn't know, but when I found out, I'd tell him. Then, one week, it was Stevie Wonder week. 'Stevie who?' Dad asked. I said 'Stevie Wonder, Dad.' And then he said, 'Who the hell is Stevie Wonder?' 'It's that black, blind fella. You know, the singer?' I told him.

Rex signs autographs during the *Canadian Idol* competition in the summer of 2005.

" 'What in the name of God do Rex know about him?' Dad said. He loved to watch it [the show]" Dwight says.

Every Tuesday night, Dwight and the Goudie clan watched *Canadian Idol*. Then, on Wednesday mornings, Roy would come out to the garage and say, "B'y, I don't think he's gonna make it tonight. He didn't do all that great. That fella Zack, he's givin' him a hard time."

Dwight told his father he worried more than the rest of them did at that point.

When Thursday morning rolled around, Roy found Dwight back at the garage. "I knew he was gonna make it!" he told Dwight.

A crowd gathered at Dwight and Tana's house the night Rex made the Top 10. While some Goudie family members were in Toronto, Roy, Ryan and Dwight were in Burlington watching the show. Whether at home or in Toronto, every time Rex sang, Tana held her breath until it was over. Her biggest fear was if he didn't make the cut, there might not be someone in Toronto to support him.

Ceilia Noble, one of Rex's best friends, remembers the times when Rex called and asked her opinion about which songs to sing for the competition. "There would be quite a discussion," she says.

But Tuesday nights in Burlington, no doubt everyone, or at least every Goudie, scattered like flies to cast their vote for Rex.

CHAPTER 12
ELVIS MUST HAVE BEEN A NEWFOUNDLANDER

A true blue Newfoundlander, Rex poses with a flag of the province for fan Arlene Kinden, in Winnipeg, Manitoba. *Submitted photo by Arlene Kinden*

A tacky Elvis bobble-head sits on a shelf in Tana's basement in Burlington.

Surrounded by Rex's guitar collection and posters plastered on the walls, Elvis fits right in.

Actually the Elvis bobble head is of good quality. His head actually bobs, unlike the faux fur Chihuahuas that fit on a car dashboard.

It was a souvenir Rex bought his mother during his trip to Graceland, which was part of the *Idol* competition.

Every time he came home from an adventure, Rex called his parents. Actually, he called — and still calls — his parents constantly.

But after the visit to Graceland, Rex made a revelation.

"Dad," he reflected, "Elvis must have been a Newfoundlander. He would go on tour and come home. Go on tour and come home. We go to Fort McMurray, then come home. Go to Fort McMurray and then come home."

Dwight laughs over his son's conclusion.

The death of a friend

Rex was in the thick of *Canadian Idol* during the summer of 2005 when his good friend Brad Shiner got killed.

It was a Sunday. He was playing video games with Melissa O'Neil when his cell phone rang.

The voice on the other end told Rex that Brad's car had gone over a cliff back in Newfoundland. He was killed instantly.

Brad was one of Rex's good buddies. They went snowmobiling together and hung out at each other's cabins.

When the news came, Rex was angry and upset, says Melissa. "He was pretty beat up over it," she says.

She tried to console him. However, it was no use.

Ceilia was in Toronto at the time. Knowing Rex as well as she did and realizing Brad was part of the gang back home, she also tried to console him. It was useless. Rex was inconsolable even to the person he considered a sister.

It was two days before that week's competition. There was no time to get to the funeral in Newfoundland and still make the show Tuesday evening. It broke Rex's heart not to be at the service, but knowing Brad the way he did, Rex knew his friend would not want him to mess up this unique shot at a music career.

Tuesday night rolled around. As difficult as it was for Rex to be on stage, somewhere inside he found the strength to get up and sing.

Melissa puts the experience into perspective. "Rex got through it because he had to. When you're young, you're totally invincible. You'll be upset and then you wake up the next day and you move on.

Practising between shows.

It's not cold, it's just the nature of the beast."

In true Goudie form, Rex never considered dropping out of the show. If anything, he dug his heels in, more determined than ever to put 'it' out there.

Despite the bumps, the negative comments and the jabs, nothing was going to stop Rex from pushing to the end.

SHARE AND SHARE ALIKE

It bothered Rex that his grandfather Roy had to drive four hours a day to have kidney dialysis. Rex even talked about doing something to help during the most competitive stages of *Canadian Idol*.

Rex knows his fans adore him.

With his newfound 'celebrity' status, Rex knew he could make a difference.

His friend and fellow Burlington native, comedian Shaun Majumder, discussed the lack of a kidney dialysis machine on the Baie Verte Peninsula numerous times.

They both wanted to see changes in the health care system back home and figured that if they pooled their talents, they could come up with something. Their aim was to raise enough money to purchase a dialysis machine for the region.

Dwight, Shaun and Rex were in downtown Toronto. As they walked, Dwight came up with a plan. "If you guys are serious about this, I'll get it started," he told the two. "But I'm going to need help. And I have a name for it right away. The SHARE Foundation. 'SHA' for Shaun and 'RE' for Rex."

The name stuck, and the three discussed more ideas they would like to include if SHARE was to fly. They wanted to do something for future generations. "And they couldn't think of anything better," Dwight says with pride.

As the summer progressed and the constant stream of Dwight-Tana-Rex supporters flowed to Toronto, Rex continued making the cut.

(Note: On Rex's first album, *Under the Lights*, the song *Call Your Name* was written with his Uncle Rex and friend Brad Shiner in mind. Rex wrote it with Rob Wells and Dave Thomson.)

Don't let the sheet music fool you. Rex plays by ear and always has. And he's pretty good too.

Rex phones home with the news he's made the Top 10.

What does one eat before appearing on national TV? Tea and toast, of course.

Getting 'in tune.'

Rex and his electric guitar.

An impromptu concert on a counter at the Deer Lake airport when Rex made the Top 10.

CHAPTER 13
THE LAST (WO)MAN STANDING

Rex's dad had a Rex Goudie hockey jersey made up just for the *Canadian Idol* competition in 2005.

Throughout the *Canadian Idol* competition, Rex had phenomenal support from both sides of his family.

From voting non-stop Tuesday nights to flying to Toronto to be there for him 'if the arse end fell outta er'' and he got voted off, Rex's family and friends were there constantly.

The support meant a lot to Rex. He was always dedicating songs to his family for one reason or another.

Aunt Trudy was the cornerstone for the Lane side of the family after her and Tana's parents died. She was there from the day Rex came home from the hospital in Tumbler Ridge right through to the day he graduated from high school. She loves her sister's boys as if they are her own.

So when Rex told her he made it to *Canadian Idol*, she said, "Rex, the only time I have off is for the last show."

Rex with his mom and dad (Dwight) take a much-needed break at the Hard Rock Café in Toronto.

"Aunt Trudy," he said, "that means I have to make it to the Top 2."

They both laughed.

On the nights when Rex was chewed out by one of the judges, she hurt for her nephew. And every Wednesday night, Trudy had people over to watch the results.

When Rex finally made the Top 2, Trudy could not 'contain' herself. "I was so excited. I jumped up and away she goes. I peed my pants. That was my experience with it. Or it could have been the excitement of going to Toronto, I don't know," she laughs.

With Rex making it to the finale, Goudies and Lanes flew from every corner of the country. Erin, Yvonne, Stacy and Terry hosted a party at their house. Stacey even made little Rex flags. Neighbours brought in food while total strangers found their way into the Lane house.

In Corner Brook, the Pepsi Centre was filled to the brim with 'Rowdy Goudie' supporters. Rex asked Erin Broderick to say a couple of kind words from there on the national television broadcast of the grand finale.

Dwight took Rex aside before the show. "I don't want you to be too disappointed if you don't win this," he told his son.

"Dad, what are you talking about?" Rex asked his father with a puzzled look. "I'm not going to be disappointed. I don't have to watch the next show from home on the chesterfield. I'm in this right to the final competition. After this, it don't matter."

Dwight was caught off-guard. "I think he had his mind made up then that he was going to do something. Whether he won it or not, he was going to give it a good shot."

On the subway in Toronto, Rex and his mom, Tana, pose for a picture after a successful day of shopping.

Aunt Trudy and Tana root for Rex during the competition.

When Melissa O'Neil was crowned *Canadian Idol*, it was obvious Rex was happy for her. He was OK with the young Albertan winning.

At the Pepsi Centre in Corner Brook, there was a silence, and then everybody stood up and applauded. No one booed Melissa.

"I was impressed," says Erin Broderick, who fought back tears after talking to Rex before the finale.

"There were thousands of people there and they were all standing up and clapping for him," she says proudly.

At the Lane house in east end St. John's, everyone was quiet when the winner was announced. You could hear a pin drop. "Nobody said a word," Yvonne says. One of the visitors started to cry. "I thought for sure Rex was going to win," Yvonne adds. "We took our things and went on."

But Ceilia wasn't so sad for the kid she called 'brother.' She was actually relieved. She felt Rex would have more freedom as an artist if he didn't win. Rex, she says, was cool with placing second.

Rex, his dad and his Uncle Mark take in a Blue Jays game.

Everything after that is a blur of activity. There was a huge all night party.

The next day was filled with media interviews and meetings.

It was time to go home and get some shut eye before Rex launched his career.

Rex and Melissa on stage after the winner was announced.

CHAPTER 14
SUCCESS CAN BE BITTER SWEET

Roy and Lillian Goudie, Rex's grandparents. Roy died on November 10, 2005.

After the *Canadian Idol* finale, Rex told his parents there was something going on the next morning. He was not quite sure what it was.

All Dwight knew was someone on stage the night before whispered to Rex that he had to be at Sony the next day at 2 p.m.

"All the next day, I was wondering, 'Geez, you're dealing with people you've never dealt with before,' " Dwight recalls. "But we did know we wanted the best for our son."

The next morning, he prepared himself mentally for what lay ahead.

At 2 p.m., the Goudies sat at Sony/BMG waiting for Rex. A young man from the finance department wandered over and asked who they were waiting for.

They told him they were Rex's parents. The man then proudly announced his hometown was Springdale, a community not far from Burlington.

"That was just crazy," Dwight muses.

When Rex arrived, he and his parents walked in the boardroom and sat at a very long table. Dwight was nervous, but Tana was more than a little curious. All Dwight knew was that he wanted Rex to get treated well.

In walked a woman. She was the president of Sony/BMG. Lisa Zbitnew stretched her hand out and said, "Well Rex, I'd like to welcome you to the Sony team."

She mentioned having an advance on his album and handed Rex an envelope.

Rex never even opened it. He just handed it to his mother. "I'll give that to the financier," he said matter-of-factly.

"There's one thing we've got to get straight before we get too far advanced," Rex stated. "It's the SHARE Foundation. It's something I firmly believe in and something I've gotten into."

As he continued, Rex more or less told the folks from Sony that if the SHARE Foundation was going to conflict with anything they wanted him to do, he was not going to be too interested in them anymore.

A Sony representative sitting at the table looked shocked. "I can't believe it. Doesn't he get excited about anything?" the man asked Dwight and Tana.

Rex never looked at his cheque. He had no idea of the amount on it. And he didn't care. Money never held much importance to him.

Rex signed the contract for his first album.

So much happened in such a short time. One of the first things Rex did with his newfound financial status was buy a new 2005, 305 horse-powered, black Mustang with red leather seats.

When Rex was growing up, a Ford Mustang was the god of cars. Now he had one. With that, a new apartment in downtown Toronto and a record deal, Rex was living his dream.

Just two months after *Canadian Idol*, Rex was in the recording studio cutting his first CD.

He worked around the clock to get the album out before Christmas. He was just three songs away from completing it when he was caught off guard by a call to Melissa's phone. No one knew Melissa and Rex were serious about each other at that point, but Dwight had sort of figured it out.

It was Dwight on the phone. He was very upset.

"Melissa, is Rex there?" Dwight asked her.

"Yes, he's asleep on the couch," she replied.

"Don't say anything right now, but Rex's grandfather just died," Dwight said.

With a deep breath, Melissa sagged under the weight of Dwight's words.

"I don't know what to do, Melissa," Dwight's almost inaudible voice said over the phone. "That's OK, Dwight, we'll figure it out," she reassured the man whose son she was in love with.

She woke Rex and handed him the phone. Melissa immediately called Rex's management team, Jim Campbell and Jen Hyland.

"I told Jim that everything on Rex's album needed to be stopped right now because there's

A four generation photo: Front row, Roy Goudie with baby Issac. Back row, Dwight, Ryan and Rex.

nothing you can do, and Rex can't do this right now," Melissa says. "And I told Jim that he needed to call the producers and tell them Rex won't be there for the next week.

"Then I called Jen and said she needed to book a flight for Rex immediately. I went back to his apartment and packed his bag."

Much older and wiser than her seventeen years, Melissa took control of the situation because she knew Rex would not be able to do it.

When she went back into his apartment, Rex was upset beyond words. When she finished packing his things, Jen e-mailed Melissa the flight itinerary. Melissa called Rex a cab, took him to the airport and sent him on his way.

In those few, short moments, Melissa's actions spoke volumes about how she felt about Rex. She would be there for him. The accident happened November 10, 2005.

That day, sixty-nine-year-old Roy was headed to Grand Falls-Windsor to have a shunt placed under his skin in preparation for the kidney dialysis he was to undertake at the hospital there.

Driving to receive treatment was something his father did not want to do, Dwight sadly recalls. "He couldn't think about moving."

This time, the drive to Grand Falls-Windsor for treatment took his life. He was the first person to die on the Burlington highway according to Dwight. About three to four inches of snow had fallen the night before. As the morning warmed up, the snow turned to a slush that made driving difficult. Roy's truck slid in a ditch and flipped over on its cab. He died instantly. Lillian was in the truck with him. Fortunately, she escaped injury.

The snow plow Mark Goudie drove to clear that stretch of road sat in a garage waiting for parts to arrive. Mark was working when the call came that a bad accident had happened.

The police officer on duty kept telling Ryan and Dwight they could not go down to the truck and retrieve Roy because it was an accident scene.

Dwight could not go down into the ditch. The sight of his father lying in the truck turned his stomach. "Ryan b'y, you gotta do something for him. You gotta go down there," he pleaded with his oldest son.

Ryan, home on leave from Voisey's Bay, headed for the truck. The police officer tried to stop him, but nothing was going to keep him from getting his pop out of the overturned truck.

Ryan is a big fella. He grabbed the door and tore it off the truck, Rex says. "That was the only damage to the truck," he adds.

The next three days saw Roy's family and friends gather to remember the father and grandfather who raised six children and built a family business in Burlington.

A white cross sits on the side of the highway on the way out of Burlington. It reminds everyone who drives by that Roy Goudie died there.

The Goudie family was under a cloak of sadness. So much had happened in such a short time. There were Tana's parents who died first, then Uncle Rex, Brad Shiner and finally Pop Goudie.

Dwight has a philosophical outlook. That which doesn't kill you makes you stronger, he notes.

When Rex returned to Toronto, he had three songs to finish. Working twenty hour days and pulling at least one all-nighter messed up his schedule up.

But that never was a question.

"When something happens to someone in the family, everything gets dropped and everyone comes running," Dwight explains.

That's just the way it is.

CHAPTER 15
MELISSA ABOUT REX

On the stage last summer, Melissa O'Neil and Rex burn the stage up during the competition.

Since Melissa O'Neil won *Canadian Idol* late in the summer of 2005, she and Rex have lived in the same building.

Though not everyone felt their enthusiasm when they proclaimed their love for each other publicly — (they just kind of blurted it out one day) — the situation they are in has forced them to lean on each other more than a normal relationship between people their age.

With Melissa and Rex, it is just the two of them and no one else in Toronto.

"I don't have my mom around to clean up after me and I can't wave a magic wand to clean this place up," says Melissa. "I have to do it myself."

WHEN THEY MET ...

Rex and Melissa have different stories. He is positive they met right at the beginning of the competition and talked and talked. She is positive they did not.

In the top 32, Rex was in group one and Melissa was in group four. "I don't really remember very much from that time anyways because everything was happening super fast," says Melissa. "I remember talking to him and hanging out in the Top 10. Once we got into the Top 10 and moved into the house together, we were a huge family."

The friendships formed. "We were living in each other's back pockets. It was tough with some of the people, but not me and Rex," Melissa continues. "Not at all."

"We hung out in the mansion watching movies and stuff."

That is when she and Rex started hanging out.

Positive.

At first, Melissa says, "we were just going through the competition. If we got through, it was, 'Awesome, sweet, let's do it again.' It's definitely a little bit of summer camp."

And then it dawned on them. "It wasn't until the Top 3, that Rex and I said, 'Oh my God. What are we going to do?' And then when we got to the Top 2… I remember the night before the results show, we didn't sleep," says Melissa.

"All we could talk about the whole night was what was going to happen to us. We were worried. If Rex wins, he's going to be in Toronto and I'm going to go home and finish school and do my thing."

"I just wanted to make sure we had it sorted out before the competition was over and not have it be some thing floating in the air. I like closure."

"I wanted to know what was going to happen and he did too. It sucked."

"We were so freaked out over what was going to happen. So when we found out that Rex was going to be doing a record, too, that pretty much blew our minds away."

The night Melissa won *Canadian Idol*, there was a party at Lot 332. "It was hilarious. I was so tired and overwhelmed. I saw all my old friends. We were just hanging out. There were some of my old teachers there. My dad was there."

It was Rex's night, too. He was so happy. He had all his friends and family there as well.

"He wouldn't let me be by myself," Melissa says. "I told Rex we had to go because we had so many interviews."

"It was 4:30 a.m. when we went back to the hotel. And he came back to my room and we hung out and talked and it was like, 'Holy crap, what just happened?' And, at the same time, we're going, 'My God, is this the last time we're going to hang out?' "

"I was so upset. My happiness was completely juxtaposed by my utter dismay with what was about to happen," Melissa recalls.

"Rex was pretty cut up about it. I was pretty fried. I was exhausted. There was no time to eat. Breakfast was scarfed down in the hallway on the way to the interview with *Canada AM*."

They both got through it though.

She had two days at home in Calgary and then she was in the studio recording her album.

Rex got to go home.

He came back to Toronto and started recording his album. And then his grandfather died in the accident.

After helping Rex through one of the toughest moments of his life, Melissa got "one of those feelings that Rex and I are going to be together for quite awhile."

Are they in love?

"Yah, you're bang on," she giggles.

CHAPTER 16
REX ABOUT MELISSA

Cuter than cute, Rex and Melissa get this photo taken while visiting Winnipeg, Manitoba while on tour. *Submitted photo by Arlene Kinden*

There's a bit of a disagreement between Rex and Melissa.

And it revolves around the time they met. Melissa says one thing. Rex definitely says another.

"We met at the Top 32. She was wearing blue jean capris and a red T-shirt with rainbow lettering. We were joking about how much she wanted to kick my butt in basketball," he insists. "And I'm right, by da Jaysez!" Rex laughs.

Then, he settles in and gets serious.

"I hope we're in for the long haul," Rex says emphatically of Melissa. "When I fall, I fall hard. And I don't fall often. So I mean this is pretty big for me. (My) last relationship was three years long. When you're seventeen or eighteen years old, that's a big thing, right?

"I couldn't get over it [the breakup] until I met Melissa. Right now I'm in a different situation all together. And I couldn't ask for any better."

Being isolated from family has forced Rex and Melissa to work out problems immediately. "That's part of it. We're in the stage now where, I'm not a great talker of relationships with whoever, but she made it very clear to me, if anything happens, let her know right away. I'm not going to leave ya. Anything we do wrong, own up to it, apologize for it, even if it's four o'clock in the morning.

"That's the way we are. As soon as I know something's wrong, I admit it, say I'm sorry and mean it."

They have a trust between them, Rex says.

"If I do something wrong, then I'm going to try and fix it. Everything I've broken, I try to fix. And that mentality carries over into a relationship. I own up to it the best I can.

"Melissa grew up in a city. I didn't. My way of fixing it is to go out on the four-wheeler and go for a ride, to think about it out in the woods.

"But in Toronto, I gotta come up with a different idea."

CHAPTER 17
LEAVING HIS MARK

If you remember the photo on page 5, Rex was in a victory stance then. Now, twenty years later, he still looks like he's on top of his game.

Rex just wanted to help wherever it was needed.

So when Roy Goudie died, it made Rex more determined to succeed in generating funds for a much-needed kidney dialysis machine for the people of the Baie Verte Peninsula.

Dwight was trying to obtain charitable organization status for the SHARE Foundation and was setting up a board of directors.

Rex was in charge of generating funds for the organization with Shaun Majumder's help.

But Rex's charitable nature did not begin with the SHARE Foundation.

Definitely not.

Rex started helping out in Burlington when he was a teen. It began with the town's recreation committee. Young Rex pushed it to make the outdoor rink operational again. Kids didn't

Emotion playing out on his face, Rex belts out a song with his trusty guitar in his hands.

have much to do in the small community. Rex believed that if the rink could have a patch of ice thrown down on it every winter, the youth could at least play some outdoor sports.

It was his way of giving back.

Once he obtained this newfound stardom, Rex felt he was in a position to make a bigger difference.

"From my standpoint — because I got to where I am because of my fans — I'm going to show my appreciation and step up and help," he says of his charitable philosophy.

That is why he got involved in the KidSport program through the Sport Newfoundland and Labrador.

"I grew up wanting to be a goalie and could never afford really good gear. My family couldn't afford to do it. It was an extra expense that we didn't really need."

As a result, he broke a lot of limbs.

As the official spokesperson for KidSport, "I wanted to be able to support the people who wanted to play hockey, but didn't have the chance because they couldn't afford it. I want to give somebody that chance," Rex says.

KidSport provides children from low income backgrounds with the means to participate in organized sports throughout the province.

"There's nothing worse than going to play and being turned down from something you want to do but can't afford," Rex says emphatically.

Rex is passionate about helping kids. That's why he became the spokesperson for another campaign called *Get Up On It*. It is an anti-drug awareness program in Newfoundland and Labrador that delivers a message with personal meaning.

"I saw drugs tear a lot of people up back home," says Rex. "I saw it turn Burlington into a hole. I don't want people to go the way I saw some of my friends go."

He watched good buddies spiral out of control. For that reason, and because he has supportive parents who kept him on the straight and narrow, Rex vowed to do what he could to encourage people not to go down a drug-infested path.

If Rex can contribute to making the world a better place, then he has accomplished what he set out to do.

And that's helping as much as he possibly can.

CHAPTER 18
THE TREEHOUSE INTERVIEW

The year following *Canadian Idol* has been one of many firsts for Rex.

One of them was getting to meet his idol, Jim Cuddy from Blue Rodeo. It was like Christmas came early for Rex. He called Dwight and, practically yelled into the telephone receiver, "I met him! I met him! And he's a nice guy, too!"

That means everything to Rex. If you're a nice guy, then you're OK in his books.

The overwhelming impact he had on the people who supported him during *Canadian Idol* also blew Rex away. For example, a retired teacher from western Canada won a substantial amount of money in a lottery and offered to pay for Rex's CD. "I don't really care if I get the money back," is what he said to Rex.

Rex was flabbergasted. He touched so many people during his time on *Canadian Idol* and never realized it.

The learning cuve has been steep as Rex has discovered the ins and outs of an industry he knew nothing about a year ago.

The day before The Outports Tour kicked off in St. John's, he sat down and shared his thoughts over a cooler filled with CheezWhiz on white bread sandwiches, raspberry jam and butter sandwiches and a few containers of chocolate milk.

The setting was a tree house at Kent's Pond in St. John's.

What follows is what Rex said as he talked about his life over the last year.

Placing second in *Canadian Idol*, Rex says, "it was scary. It was a dream come true, beyond all beliefs. [Music] was something that was always in the back of my mind. It was something, other than mechanic work, that I was passionate about.

"It was something I loved to do.

"The thing is, I've got to stick with it. If you believe you can do something, then you're going to do it. You can pretty much do anything you want to do.

However, "I always try to please everybody all the time. That's my problem. I keep trying to do that. I've been trying to do that all my life. It hurts me if somebody doesn't like what I'm doing. I can't stand to see anyone hurting because of me, even if it's in the smallest way.

"I try to please everybody and make everybody happy.

"In any relationship, I try to make my parents happy and the person I'm with happy. A lot of the time I do. But a relationship has to be two ways. There has to be compromise there somewhere.

"But in life, it may sound harsh to say, you've got to look out for yourself. You've got to do what's going to make you happy. And if what's going to make you satisfied is knowing that everyone around you is taken care of, that's what you go for.

"I learned to be confident in myself. This is what I want to do. If I'm content myself, it's easier to make other people happy.

"I'll admit, I have changed a little bit. I've got a different appreciation of people and how influential people are. There are people in life: your parents, your siblings, your cousins. There are the people you work with: your managers, music directors, presidents of companies. Whoever you deal with, you have to make relationships with everybody. Your fans, you've got to make a relationship with your fans in this business. Fans are the biggest thing.

"But that being said, you can't stretch yourself too thin between all these people. I was trying to do some Christmas shopping in Corner Brook. I think everyone came out to the Plaza there to get an autograph.

"I couldn't move. That's spreading yourself too thin. That's when you kind of got to be selfish. That's when you hear the bad stories of some people, you know?

"People do too much. But you've got to take everything in stride, even everything out.

"Sometimes you get the weird side of things. You don't have your own life anymore. You've got to be so accommodating sometimes that you don't have your own life.

"There's got to be respect in every relationship, even with fans. I told all my good friends, 'If you ever ask me for an autograph for yourself, I'm gonna smack ya. I won't hesitate. Don't ask me. For your cousin, I don't mind. But for you, yourself, don't ever ask me.' Because they knew me before.

"And now, they shouldn't be there asking for an autograph and saying, 'Oh, I'm hanging out with Rex Goudie. I'm hangin' around with 'Box' and a few other names.' That's what I pride myself on. My true friends are still my true friends.

"I've got a lot better appreciation for the music industry now and touring because I've had a taste of it. I've worked as hard as anybody else. It comes in spurts though."

Rex wants to do his own style of music so when the first couple of chords are played, you'll recognize it as a Rex Goudie song, like you do for artists such as Bryan Adams and AC/DC.

"I try to be real. I worry about that.

"After *Idol*, I'm trying to put myself in a place where I can be comfortable with it and in it for a long time. I'm trying to gain the respect I need . What I want to be is a Canadian version of an icon of rock music. I want to do what I love and still be recognized for it.

"I want to reach people with lyrics and performances, but I still want to reach the younger generation, not with pop music, but with rock and roll, heavier music.

"Classic rock is where it's at. The stuff that's on today, to be honest with ya, I don't think any of it is going to be around in the next ten years. Look at the Backstreet Boys. Those guys had an amazing career. But you should be able to shift. Madonna has been able to do that. She keeps reinventing herself over and over again.

"Then there are the ones [who] do the same thing over and over again, like AC/DC, Metallica. They're critically acclaimed for it. Because that's what they do. That's what they're good at. And they're the personable people.

"I want to be 'that' guy. 'That' guy is the type of person that everybody was amazed by at some point. But when it comes to the nitty gritty of it, he's no different than anybody else."

After rooting around in Rex Goudie's life for the last few months, I can honestly say, he is 'that guy.'

In the eyes of Newfoundlanders and Labradorians, Rex is such a positive role model. From the children who worship him to the little old ladies who adore him, Rex is 'idolized' not just for his incredible singing talent, but in the way he puts himself out there and keeps giving back to his community and his province. He's not just an idol, he's an icon. Newfoundland loves him because he loves it back with intensity that is often lost in the shuffle of life. He's so proud of where he's from. And he loves — no, adores — his family.

But coming from a small town in Newfoundland has given Rex the foundation he needs to be successful in anything he does. So whether he's turning wrenches or singing on stage, Rex will be successful.

Because good guys do finish first. And Rex certainly is one of them.

LITTLE KNOWN FACTS

Rex, on the beach with "his boy," nephew Issac.

- Rex likes CheezWhiz sandwiches on white bread.
- He loves chocolate milk.
- He has allergies to dry grass, oil paint and long-haired dogs.
- He doesn't eat his crusts.
- His favorite foods include any kind of cereal, chicken wings, and jiggs dinner.
- He wears a size medium T-shirt.
- Issac, his brother Ryan's little boy, is the apple of his eye.
- He and Melissa exchanged promise rings and he wears his on his left ring finger.
- Most of his friends are girls.
- He says he's not romantic. He bought Melissa a camera for Christmas.
- He drove to Calgary in his car to surprise Melissa for her Grade Twelve graduation (but he's not romantic?).

- Growing up, his parents used to call him 'Mario' because he jumped from one piece of furniture to the next.
- He loves beagles.
- The white hat that became his trademark cost about $5. It was the best $5 he has ever spent, he says.
- Rex's musical influences include Jim Cuddy, Kris Kristopherson, Bruce Springsteen, Dave Grohl, Tom Petty, Johnny Cash, Charlie Major, John Fogerty, Eric Clapton and Bryan Adams.
- He hates sleazy media interviews where the reporter slams him or Melissa.
- His Ford Mustang is his favorite type of car.
- He loves Bombardier snowmobiles.
- He thinks his Dad is the greatest Newfoundlander who ever lived.
- If Rex can't play music, he'll go back to turning wrenches.
- He's a picky eater.
- If he could go anywhere in the world, he'd visit Beaumont Hamel in France.
- He doesn't like most of the songs on his album.
- He HATES the name S _ _Y REX_. (He made the author promise not to use the words!)
- He despises 'Rexperts.'
- Rex's definition of a true man: He's not afraid to admit failure; he's not afraid to admit when he's wrong and not afraid to know when he's right.
- When he falls for a girl, he falls hard.

HAVIN' A GAB WITH REX (Q & A SECTION)

These questions were sent by Rex's fans through the on-line forum created through his web-site, www.rexgoudie.ca. Some folks are from his fan club, The Rexinators, while others are simply his fans.

The questions were asked one sunny afternoon in a treehouse on Kent's Pond in St. John's. We chatted for hours and I got to know Rex just a little more than I already did. We told jokes and laughed a lot.

To the fans who emailed their questions to me, thank you. Involving you in this book was as important as interviewing Rex.

While not all your questions were asked, I believe the ones that I did get to were the very best. I hope you're not disappointed and enjoy reading Rex's answers as much as I enjoyed asking him your questions.

From Stephanie in Brigus, NL.

Q. How old were you when you had your first kiss?
Rex. Grade eight. Karla Shiner. It was on the lips.

Fan question:

Q. How do you feel when your fans rally behind one fan in order to get in contact with you in support of that fan?
Rex. That's an amazing story how they all got behind Alana like that. She's an American fan. She apparently went paralyzed. She's about sixteen. Everybody sent something from home. People were trying to contact me [and tell me her story].
Some people did contact me and didn't believe it was me. That's how dedicated they were.
They were just trying to do something for somebody else. But to see people put themselves through that for the sake of helping out one of their [online] friends, that's true. That's pretty much what I'm about. I agree with that.
I did everything I could for her. I tried to make up a video message for her with the cameras at Sony/BMG. [I] Got a great big poster to send down to her. [I did] whatever I could to make her feel better. It took awhile to get it all arranged but we finally sent it down to her.
It's really touching to see that kind of support. It reminds me of my family. If anything happens to any one of us, the whole family just surrounds everybody. It's like a circling of the wagons.

Note: This was taken from an e-mail from Glenda, a Rex fan and Alana supporter, and explains it a bit further.
"There's a young girl named Alana, who lives in California. She is a big fan of Rex. One day,

she was suddenly struck down with a paralyzing illness. She is now paralyzed from the neck down and on a respirator. Rexinat[ors] knew they didn't see her [on line] and didn't know why. Then her boyfriend posted a message about what happened. He has since posted several videos from Alana. The way the Rex fans have rallied together to send her things and contact Rex has been unbelievable."

From Heather, in Walkerton, ON.

Q. If you and Melissa ever broke up, would you continue with your singing career?

Rex. That's a tough question. I don't know. If it ever happens (knocks on a piece of wood), I'll deal with it then.

Fan question:

Q. When is it you feel the happiest and why?

Rex. When I'm home on my skidoo or underneath a truck. There's lots of times when I'm the happiest, I'm comfortable and I can relax. And I can only do that when I'm either home or away from people who are trying to pull you around. [I'm happy] when someone says, you've worked hard, take a break. We feel you deserve it. My place to relax is a little sixteen by sixteen cabin on Long Pond Ridge that you can only get to by snow machine.

From Elizabeth in St. John's, NL.

Q. If you had three wishes, what would they be and why?

Rex. Wish one, if I could do the same thing I'm doing now, but live home. Wish two, that I could make everybody happy. Wish three, it's kind of awkward, but wish three would be that I could bring back the people I've lost and spend a little bit more time with them, just a day. But then, that would leave me wishing for one more day, and one more day.

Fan question:

Q. If you could go anywhere in the world, where would it be?

Rex. Go to Beaumont Hamel, France. There's so much history over there. So many Newfoundlanders went over there and died [World War I].

From Mary L.

Q. What has being a contestant on *Canadian Idol* personally taught you?

Rex. Whew. Dedication, partly. How to pace myself. Plus, not everything is so glamorous [as it is] on T.V.

From Emily in Fredericton, NB.

Q. What is your favorite car?

Rex. Ford Mustang. I got it because it's a Ford Mustang. They finally brought back a sensible car for a Mustang.

Fan question:

Q. What are your thoughts on the National Hockey League on the past season?

Rex. It was interesting because with some of the new rules, they proved the game could be fast. It proved that the game could not rely on zero-zero games in defense anymore, hence the Calgary Flames losing in the first round. On the bad side, you had some weird penalties like clearing the puck over the boards when you're in a defensive zone. Not many people tried to do that. A lot of times, it's a reaction. What we were always taught in minor hockey, if you're pressured, dump the puck off the boards. And if it just happens to get over the boards, now a days, a fella gets a penalty for it. And to be honest, a lot of the games in the Stanley Cup finals this year were [decided] by dumb penalties like that being called.

From Della-Lynn, Port-au-Port Peninsula, NL.

Q. Do you have any idea how the song, *Call your name* impacts your fans?

Rex. It's a pretty intense song. There were some pretty intense feelings that went into that song. I cried when I wrote it. It speaks about two pretty influential people in my life. It talks about my Uncle Rex, who was around when Dad was away working, and Brad Shiner, who was an old friend of mine. I grew up idolizing what he could do with a machine. The guy was a genius. It drew a lot of emotion out of me and gave me a chance to pay tribute to the people I never really had a chance to tell how I felt about them.

From Pam in Harry's Harbour, NL.

Q. If there was one thing you could change about yourself, what would it be?

Rex. One thing I'm trying to change right now, I'm trying to be in better shape. I'm trying to work out. I'm not a really strong fella and I don't carry a big presence, 'cause I'm not a bigger fella like Ryan [Goudie]. It's like Shaun Majumder told me. 'When you know you feel good about yourself and you're in good shape and you can handle yourself well, you carry a lot more confidence.' And that's the truth of it. As soon as I get into the next apartment, I'm going to start working out.

From Bethany in Toronto, ON.

Q. When you were on *Canadian Idol*, was there a night you felt, for sure, you were going home? Why?

Rex. I wasn't cocky about it. I had good luck so far and when was the luck gonna run out? That's the thing. I don't base everything on luck but it was luck that I got in there for the auditions that day. But I think about that a lot. I didn't know how far I was going to make it. I didn't know how people were gonna vote. You couldn't judge by anything. Do the best you could and put everything out there on the stage. That's what I thought every week.

From Sheldon in Grand Falls-Windsor, NL.

Q. What's your most embarrassing moment since *Canadian Idol*?
Rex. Not winning and having this question come up.

From Arlene in Winnipeg, MB.

Q. Do you remember the fan who brought you the present from home (Newfoundland) at the concert in Winnipeg?
R. Yes I do remember her and I did receive it.

From Jane in Conception Bay South, NL.

Q. Do you find it hard to be true to yourself and your family, not letting yourself get in over your head?
Rex. Not too bad because my family is there to tell me when I'm getting in over my head. They say to me, 'Now I think you're getting a little bit too far in now, calm down.'

From Anne in Hamilton, ON.

Q. Are you writing any country music?
Rex. Any song can be made into a country song. I like Alan Jackson and those guys. My thing was I tried to lean more towards more edgy stuff. Along those same lines, you could still write a good song without it having it be heavy. Country's too classified. Most country [music] today is too pop. Country music used to be Alan Jackson, George Strait and Hank Williams Senior. Not even Garth Brooks is country music [these days]. The day that Trace Adkins put out the song, *Honky Tonk Badonkadonk*, Hank Williams and every dead country writer — Johnny Cash and a whole lot of 'em — rolled over in their graves.

From Stephanie in Mississauga, ON.

Q. If you could meet any three people in the world, living or dead, who would they be? Why?
Rex. Hmm. Living or dead? I'd meet Hitler and ask him 'Why?'
Johnny Cash and pat him on the back. He was a musical genius and he had the courage to get what he wanted in music. And then he went after June Carter like crazy. True love story. That's another big thing.
The other person I'd meet would probably be, Felix Potvin. Felix Potvin is why I became a goalie. I'd just like to have a chat even if it's to shoot the breeze, it would be pretty cool.

From Cristianne in West Pubnico, NS.

Q. If you could duet with anyone, dead or alive, who would it be?
Rex. I liked to do a small cover with a song like, *Till I gain control again*, with Jim Cuddy or *Cocaine Blues* with Johnny Cash.

From: Jessica in Sault Ste. Marie, ON.

Q. Who is your most memorable fan and what did they do to make themselves memorable?
Rex. Wow, that's kind of an awkward question to answer. Actually, Alana. The fact that she inspired so many people to get behind her so much, I'll always remember that.

Fan question:

Q. What do you miss most [from] before *Canadian Idol*?
Rex. Work and getting up in the morning, knowing that you're going to work, and knowing you've done a fine day of work.

From Lisa C.

Q. How has all this instant success impacted you and your family so far?
Rex. It's not awkward on the family because though I've gone away, I'm still around. The fact that they've got every DVD from the show helps a lot. I had a lot of support from them. I wouldn't have been able to do it without their support. I know they're there behind me. They kept me real. Even though I was on *Idol*, or on the phone talking and asking how everyone was doing, I wouldn't have been able to do it without them.

From Princess Kristina in ON.

Q. Do you have a favorite song to perform live and why?
Rex. I used to sing *Barrett's Privateers*, turn the guitar over and pat out the drum beat on the back of 'er singing at the Breezeway. That was a lot of fun because everybody started singing it. It was wicked.

From Laurie in Oshawa, ON.

Q. Why is it every time I turn on my air conditioning in my Kia van, it shuts your CD off? I hate to choose between sweltering for an hour in Toronto traffic and going Rexless for the whole ride.
Rex. That is a bad ground wire. I don't know exactly where they are but you've got a dirty ground somewhere and when you turn on the air conditioning, it's messing up the CD player. Dad's pickup does the same thing.

From Rhonda in Mount Pearl, NL.

Q. What do you have planned next?
Rex. I'm starting writing tomorrow. The first formal writing session starts tomorrow.

Fan question:

Q. Is there a date of release for new CD?
Rex. They're aiming for December 5, but I'm not confident it'll be done in time.

Fan question:

Q. What do you think of people who scalp your tickets?
Rex. I don't think it's right for scalpers to be selling tickets for high prices. They go to the box office, they go early, get all the good seats and if they don't resell those tickets, then those seats aren't filled. The tickets are still sold but the seats are empty. It doesn't look good. It's also illegal. The scalpers buy the tickets, but it's not fair to everyone else.

Fan question:

Q. How do you describe yourself?
Rex. A mechanic from Burlington, Newfoundland. It's a bit hard to describe yourself. It comes off as being self centred and I don't like doing it.

Fan question:

Q. Do you plan on making music a full time career or do you have a back up plan?
Rex. I always give it the best that I can. I'm going to try and stick with this for as long as I possibly can.

Fan question:

Q. What's a favorite thing you like to do in your down time?
Rex. Driving in my car with Melissa or playing hockey.

Fan question:

Q. Who's your favorite Newfoundlander?
Rex. My father. He's full of Newfoundland spirit, this fella. He works as hard as he possibly can, all day long. And he comes home and relaxes in the evenings. He believes in everything that is Newfoundland.

From Melissa M.

Q. Have you taken any singing lessons?
Rex. Some but not long term.

From Elizabeth in St. John's, NL.

Q. If you could do anything in the world, what would it be?
Rex. Play hockey on the ice at Maple Leaf Gardens.

From Mary L.

Q. What was your most embarrassing moment on *Canadian Idol*?
Rex. Anytime I had to dance. Rock and roll isn't about dancing. It's about jumpin' off of stuff and getting everybody goin.'

From Kayla L.

Q. Out of all the songs on your CD, which one do you like the most playing live?
R. *Strong Enough*. I like playing it live.

Fan question:

Q. What was the only thing that made you fall in love with Melissa?
R. The only thing? There's more than one thing. The biggest thing would be how I get along with her. She's so easy to talk to and good to get along with. I found her very easy to fall for.

Fan question:

Q. What do you look for in a girl?
Rex: Smile and a personality.

From Elecia in Sarnia, ON.

Q. What was it like to tour across Canada for the 'Let it go' Tour since you had never been off The Rock before?
Rex. It was kind of exhausting at some points. We had obligations and interviews with the press and things got mixed up. We didn't get to eat because of our obligations and we went on stage hungry. And that sucks. That only happened once but that's the worst example. But to go on stage with an empty stomach and bronchitis. I guess it was from not looking after myself. I take a lot better care of myself now.

Reba , the Rexinator Fan Club leader, #73 misreba, wrote this poem for Rex.

"You and I are a face in the crowd,
We are here to see our one desire.
We scream, we rave, we sing along,
But we are not strangers, no sir,
We are "Rexinators".
We are dear to one another and here,
In this place all have one cause;
To vote for, request and even 'breathe' Rex Goudie…

Thank you everyone for your questions. I hope you feel like you played a part in this project as much as I felt you did.

…Kim

Rex's fans mean a lot to him. On his way for a hair-cut the morning of the kick off to the Outports Tour in St. John's, June 23, he stopped and signed Holly Loder's white baseball cap while she sat in line wait-ing for Hilary Duff concert tickets to go on sale at Mile One Stadium.

Rex doesn't just have one hockey jersey. He has dozens. These are only just a few that call his bed-room home.

Rex's closet was a lot emptier before he started *Canadian Idol*. Now, there's no room left for much of anything.

Neat and tidy, Rex's bedroom in Burlington holds all that's dear to him. His mom and dad jokingly call it "the shrine" because it contains everything from the *Canadian Idol* experience and then some.

A LETTER FROM A FAN

Hello. I would like to share my story of meeting a true *Canadian Idol*.

Earlier this week, I attended the YORK Street Tim Horton's late in the evening. At the counter was an older gentleman who had ordered a sandwich and a drink. Immediately behind him was a young man around the age of 18. When the man who had ordered was unable to pay for his order with a debit card and apparently had no funds on his person, the young man offered to pay for his meal. Without hesitation the young gentleman presented a $20.00 bill and paid for the man. I later learned that the gentleman was from Arkansas and was unaware of the "cash only" policy of Tim Hortons. He informed me that he was overwhelmed by the generosity of a man so young in his years.

After receiving my order, I approached the generous Canadian and offered to repay what he had spent on the sandwich and drink. He flatly refused my offer and said it had been his pleasure to help out. At that point, I was informed by a friend that this young man was *Canadian Idol*, Rex.

It is a pleasure to inform you that this young Idol participant was generous without a hint of arrogance and was wanting no recognition for his act of kindness. He was genuinely happy to just assist someone in need. As far as I am concerned, this young man has proven himself to be a wonderful role model for the Canadian youth and is already considered an Idol by my standards.

Rex was accompanied by Diego and Giselle. The three of them were a picture of politeness, kindness and appropriateness. It is with complete sincerity that I say that they make me proud of our Canadian youth.

I wish the three of them the best of luck and will definitely be watching this Tuesday evening and plan to place my vote accordingly.

Sincerely,

Christine Bender
Timmins, Ontario

ABOUT THE AUTHOR

Rex Goudie: Idolized is Kim Kielley's third book. She has also written *A Boat Called Hipjoint* and *Angels and Miracles: True Stories.* Kielley brings over twenty years of writing experience to her first book with Creative Book Publishing. She also is the associate editor of *the ex/press* in St. John's, Newfoundland.

Acknowledgements

Thanks to everyone who made this project possible. Special thanks to CTV for lending us some photos: Dwight and Tana; Mark, Trudy, Toby, Yvonne, Terry, Stacey, Erin, Garland, Erin Broderick, Ceilia, Lillian, Alonso, Donna, Steve, Kerri, Joanne, Todd, Dana, Sandy, Carol, Dad, John, Joe, Josh, all of the fans who wrote in and Rex.

...Kim